Stories for Six-Year-Olds

also edited by Sara and Stephen Corrin

retold by Sara and Stephen Corrin
Illustrated by Errol Le Cain
MRS FOX'S WEDDING

ff

STORIES FOR 6-YEAR-OLDS

Edited by
Sara and Stephen Corrin

faber and faber
LONDON · BOSTON

First published in 1967 by Faber and Faber Ltd., 3 Queen Square, London WC1N 3AU. Reprinted 1968, 1972, 1973, 1976 and 1980. First paperback edition published in the United States in 1989 by Faber and Faber Inc., 50 Cross Street, Winchester, MA 01890.

Library of Congress Cataloging-in-Publication Data

Stories for six year olds.
    Summary: A collection of traditional and modern stories to be read aloud.
    1. Children's stories. 2. Tales. (1. Short stories. 2. Fairy tales. 3. Folklore) I. Corrin, Sara. II. Corrin, Stephen. III. Title: Stories for 6 year olds.
PZ5.S88165   1989   (E)   88-33471
ISBN 0-571-12959-5

Printed in the United States of America

Contents

———————————✳———————————

Contents

6

Contents

Acknowledgements

————————————————*————————————————

We are most grateful to the undermentioned publishers and authors for permission to include the following stories:

Messrs. Geo. G. Harrap and Co. Ltd. for *The Discontented Pig* from *Educating by Story-Telling* by K. D. Cather.

Messrs. Geo. G. Harrap and Co. Ltd. and Houghton Mifflin Co. for *The Adventures of the Little Field Mouse* from *Stories to Tell to Children* by Sara Cone Bryant, published in Great Britain by Geo. G. Harrap and Co. Ltd.

Messrs. Faber and Faber Ltd. and Diana Ross for *The Story of the Little Red Engine*.

The Lutterworth Press and Diana Ross for *The Enormous Apple Pie*.

John Murray (Publishers) Ltd. for *The Little Jackal and the Alligator* from *Old Deccan Days* by Mary Frere.

Rupert Hart-Davis Ltd. for *Silly Simon* from the series *First Folk Tales* by Mollie Clarke.

Frederick Muller Ltd. for *The Mouse Bride* from *Indian Fairy Tales* by Lucia Turnbull.

Thomas Nelson and Sons Ltd. for *The Laughing Dragon* by Richard Wilson and for *Oeyvind and his Goat* by Björnsterne Björnsen, both taken from *The Youngest Omnibus* edited by Rosalind Vallance.

Acknowledgements

W. and A. K. Johnson and G. W. Bacon Ltd. for *Mr. Buffin and Harold Trotter* by Robert Hartman.

Ella Monckton for *The Cow, the Duck and the Pig.*

Basil Blackwell and Mott Ltd. for *The Snow-Man* by Mabel Marlowe.

Elizabeth Clark for *The Old Woman who Lived in a Vinegar-bottle.*

The Society of Authors as the literary representatives of the Estate of the late Rose Fyleman for *The Broom* by Rose Fyleman.

Messrs. Faber and Faber Ltd. for *Tim Rabbit's Umbrella* from *The Adventures of No Ordinary Rabbit* by Alison Uttley.

We should also like to express our thanks to Miss Eileen H. Colwell and her staff at the Hendon Library for their enormous help and to Miss Phyllis Hunt of Faber and Faber for ready advice at all times.

A Word to the Story-teller

———

————————————*————————————

The reception given to our *Stories for Seven-Year-Olds* has encouraged us to compile a similar volume for the sixes and other young readers.

Can stories really be so rigidly classified as to justify the title *Stories for Six-Year-Olds*? Most teachers will say that they can, which does not imply, of course, that, the same stories will not be of interest to other age groups. It means simply that every age has differing emotional and intellectual requirements and that there are some stories very much more suited than others to meet these requirements. Each age-range—and each child within this range—will draw from the story at different levels, according to need; so that in a class of forty six-year-olds one is catering for forty individuals at forty different levels. And yet the whole class will sit entranced, linked by some magic spell.

The present volume contains mainly traditional stories, including several by the brothers Grimm, freely adapted, and some from this century. We have roamed far and wide for our tales but there is also a goodly sprinkling of English stories. The collection has been tried out and proved its worth with classes of six-year-olds—as well as with individual children. It will help, of course, if the teacher reads them in such a way as to convey her own enthusiasm for them to the child. This goes for the parent, too, as well as for the aunt or elder sister. The story-teller should not be afraid of adding a little trimming here and there, for these stories are highly condensed affairs. Sometimes a word or phrase may be adapted to suit the capacity or temperament of the particular listener. And above all, the story-teller must not fight shy of dramatising—dramatic tension is the one thing which young people find irresistible. All this is safely within the story-telling tradition, for over the many years that traditional tales have been handed down they have been added to and embellished in all sorts of ways. But never, of course, beyond recognition. The basic themes remain; we find them appearing in various guises in all parts of the world.

The Old Woman who Lived in a Vinegar-bottle

---------------------------------*---------------------------------

O nce upon a time there was an Old Woman who lived
in a Vinegar-bottle; (she had a little ladder to go in
and out by). She lived there for a great many years,
but after a time she grew discontented (and wouldn't you—if
you lived in a Vinegar-bottle?). And one day she began to
grumble, and she grumbled so loud that a Fairy, who was
passing by, heard her.

"Oh dear! Oh dear! Oh dear!" she said. "I oughtn't to live

The Old Woman who Lived in a Vinegar-bottle

in a Vinegar-bottle. 'Tis a shame, so it is, 'tis a shame. I ought to live in a nice little white house, with pink curtains at the windows and roses and honeysuckle growing over it, and there ought to be flowers and vegetables in the garden and a pig in a sty. So there ought. 'Tis a shame, so it is, 'tis a shame."

Well, the Fairy was sorry for her (and wouldn't you be sorry for a person who lived in a Vinegar-bottle?). And she said, "Well, never you mind. But when you go to bed tonight, just you turn round three times, and when you wake up in the morning you'll see what you'll see!"

So the Old Woman went to bed in the Vinegar-bottle and she turned round three times. (I don't know how there was room to do it.) And when she woke up in the morning, she was in a little white bed in a room with pink curtains. And she jumped out of bed and ran across the room and pulled aside the pink curtains and looked out of the window. And it was a little white house, with roses and honeysuckle, and there was a garden with flowers and vegetables, and she could hear a pig—grunting in the sty!

Well, the Old Woman was pleased. But she never thought to say "thank you" to the Fairy.

Well, the Fairy she went East and she went West, and she went North and she went South; and one day she came back to where the Old Woman was living in the little white house with pink curtains at the windows, and roses and honeysuckle—and flowers and vegetables in the garden—and the pig in the sty. And the Fairy said to herself, "I'll just go and take a look at her. She will be pleased."

But do you know, as the Fairy passed by the Old Woman's window, she could hear the Old Woman talking to herself, and what do you think she was saying? "Oh! 'tis a shame," said the Old Woman, "'tis a shame. So it is, 'tis a shame. Why should I live in a poky little cottage? Other folks live in little red brick houses on the edge of the town where they can watch who goes by to market. Why shouldn't I live in a little red brick house on the edge of the town and see the folks going by to market? And I'm getting too old to do my own work. I ought to have a little maid to wait on me. So I did. Oh! 'tis a shame, 'tis a shame, 'tis a shame.''

Well, the Fairy was disappointed because she did hope she would have been pleased. But she said, "Well, never you mind. When you go to bed tonight, just you turn round three times, and when you wake up in the morning you'll see what you'll see!''

So the Old Woman went to bed in the little white house with the pink curtains at the windows and the roses and honeysuckle —and the flowers and vegetables in the garden—and the pig in the sty. And she turned round three times. And when she woke up in the morning—someone was standing by the bed, saying, "Please, mum, I've brought you a cup o' tea.'' And when she opened her eyes and looked, there was a little maid to help her do her work; and she'd brought the Old Woman a cup of tea to drink before she got out of bed. And when the Old Woman had drunk her tea, she got up and looked out of the window. And it was a little red brick house, and it was on the edge of the town, and she could see the folk going by to market!

Well, the Old Woman was pleased. But she never thought to say "Thank you" to the Fairy.

Well, the Fairy she went East and she went West, and she went North and she went South; and one day she came back to where the Old Woman was living in the little red brick house, on the edge of the town, and where she could see the folks going by to market. And the Fairy said to herself, "I'll just go and take a look at her. She will be pleased!''

But do you know, when the Fairy stood on the Old Woman's door-step, she could hear (through the key-hole) the Old

The Old Woman who Lived in a Vinegar-bottle

Woman talking to herself. (The Fairy wasn't listening at the key-hole. It was just as high as her ear, and she couldn't help hearing.) And what do you think she was saying? "Oh! 'tis a shame," said the Old Woman, "'tis a shame, so it is, 'tis a shame. Why should I live in a little house, when other folks live in a big house in the middle of the town, with white steps up to the door, and men and maids to wait on them, and a carriage and pair to go driving in? Why shouldn't I live in a big house, in the middle of the town, with white steps up to the door, and men and maids to wait on me, and a carriage and pair to go driving in? 'Tis a shame, 'tis a shame, so it is, 'tis a shame!"

Well, the Fairy was disappointed, because she did hope that she would have been pleased. But she said, "Well, never you mind. When you go to bed tonight, just you turn round three times, and when you wake up in the morning you'll see what you'll see!"

So the Old Woman went to bed that night in the little red brick house on the edge of the town, where she could see the folks going by to market, and she turned round three times, and when she woke up in the morning—she was in the grandest bed she had ever seen! It had brass knobs at the top and brass knobs at the bottom; the Old Woman had never seen a bed like that before. And when she got up and looked out of the window, it was a big house, and it was in the middle of the town, and there were white steps up to the door and men and maids to wait on her, and a carriage and pair to go driving in.

Well, the Old Woman was pleased. But she never thought to say "Thank you" to the Fairy.

Well, the Fairy she went East and she went West, and she went North and she went South, and one day she came back to the town where the Old Woman was living in the big house, in the middle of the town, with white steps up to the door and men and maids to wait on her, and a carriage and pair to go driving

The Old Woman who Lived in a Vinegar-bottle

in. And the Fairy said to herself, "I'll just go and take a look at her. She will be pleased."

But do you know, as soon as the Fairy stood inside the Old Woman's door, she could hear the Old Woman talking to herself, and what do you think she was saying? "Oh! 'tis a shame," said the Old Woman, "'tis a shame, so it is, 'tis a shame. Look at the Queen," said the Old Woman, "sitting on a gold throne, and living in a Palace, with a gold crown on her head, and red velvet carpet to walk on. Why shouldn't I be a Queen and sit on a gold throne and live in a Palace, with a gold crown on my head and a red velvet carpet to walk on? 'Tis a shame, 'tis a shame, so it is, 'tis a shame."

Well the Fairy was disappointed because she did think she would have been pleased. But she said, "Well-l-l-l, never you mind. When you go to bed tonight, just you turn round three times, and when you wake up in the morning you'll see what you'll see."

So the Old Woman went to sleep in the grand bed with the brass knobs at the top and the brass knobs at the bottom, in the big house, in the middle of the town, with white steps up to the door, and men and maids to wait on her, and a carriage and pair to go driving in. And she turned round three times, and when she woke up in the morning—she was in the grandest bed that ever was seen, with a red satin coverlet, and there was red velvet carpet by the side of the bed, and a gold crown on a table all ready to put on when she dressed. So the Old Woman got up and dressed and put on the gold crown, and walked on the red velvet carpet, and there was a gold throne to sit on. And the Old Woman was pleased. But she never thought to say "Thank you" to the Fairy.

Well, the Fairy she went East and she went West, and she went North and she went South, and one day she came back to the town where the Old Woman was living in the Palace, with

The Old Woman who Lived in a Vinegar-bottle

a gold crown on her head and a gold throne to sit on and a red velvet carpet to walk on. And the Fairy said to herself, "I'll just go and take a look at her. She will be pleased."

So she walked right in at the Palace door, and up the red velvet stairs till she came to where the Old Woman was sitting on a gold throne with a gold crown on her head. And as soon as the Old Woman saw the Fairy she opened her mouth and what do you think she said? "Oh! 'tis a shame," said the Old Woman, "'tis a shame, so it is, 'tis a shame. This throne is most uncomfortable, the crown is too heavy for my head and there's a draught down the back of my neck. This is a most inconvenient house. Why can't I get a home to suit me? 'Tis a shame, 'tis a shame, so it is, 'tis a shame."

"Oh, very well," said the Fairy. "If all you want is just a house to suit you, when you go to bed tonight, just you turn round three times, and when you wake up in the morning you'll see," said the Fairy.

So the Old Woman went to bed that night in the Palace, in the big bed with the red satin coverlet and the red velvet carpet by the side of the bed, and the gold crown on a table all ready to put on in the morning. And she turned round three times (there was plenty of room to do it).

And when she woke up in the morning—she was BACK IN THE VINEGAR-BOTTLE. And she stayed there the rest of her life!

The Snow-man

———————————*———————————

A snow-man once stood upon a hill, with his face towards the sunset. A very fine snow-man he was, as tall as a soldier, and much fatter. He had two pieces of glass for eyes, and a stone for a nose, and a piece of black wood for a mouth, and in his hand he held a stout, knobbly club.

But he had no clothes at all, not even a hat, and the wind on the top of that hill was as bitter as wind could be.

"How cold I am! I am as cold as ice," said the snow-man. "But that red sky looks warm." So he lifted his feet from the ground, and went tramp, tramp, tramping down the slope towards the setting sun.

Very soon he overtook a gipsy woman, who was wearing a bright red shawl. "Ha, that looks warm! I must have it," thought the snow-man. So he went up to the gipsy woman and he said, "Give me that red shawl."

"No, indeed! I cannot spare it on this wintry day," answered the gipsy. "I am cold enough as it is."

"Cold!" shouted the snow-man in a very growlish voice. "Are you as cold as I am, I wonder! Are you cold inside as well as outside? Are you made of ice, through and through and through?"

"No, I suppose not," mumbled the gipsy, who was getting hot with fright.

"Then give me your red shawl this moment, or I shall strike you with my stout, knobbly club."

Then the gipsy took off her red shawl, grumbling all the time, and gave it to the snow-man. He put it round his shoulders, without a word of thanks, and went tramp, tramp, tramping down the hill. And the shivering gipsy woman followed behind him.

Presently the snow-man overtook a ploughboy who was wearing his grandmother's long, red woollen mittens.

"Ha! They look warm! I must have them," thought the snow-man. So he went up to the ploughboy and he said, "Give me those red woollen mittens."

"No, indeed!" said the ploughboy. "They belong to my grandmother. She lent them to me because my fingers were so cold."

"Cold!" shouted the snow-man, in a very roarish voice. "Are your fingers as cold as mine, I wonder! Are your hands and arms frozen into ice, through and through and through?"

"No, I suppose not," mumbled the ploughboy.

"Then give me those red mittens, this moment, or I shall strike you with my stout, knobbly club."

So the ploughboy drew off the warm mittens, grumbling all the time, and the snow-man put them on, without a word of thanks. Then he went tramp, tramp, tramping down the hill. And the gipsy and the ploughboy followed him.

After a while he overtook a tame pirate, wearing a pirate's thick red cap, with a tassel dangling down his back.

"Ha! That looks warm! I must have it," said the snow-man. So he went up to the tame pirate and he said, "Give me that red tassel cap."

"No, indeed!" said the pirate. "A nice cold in the head I should get if I did."

"Cold in the head!" shouted the snow-man, in a very thunderish voice. "Is your head as cold as mine, I wonder! Are your brains made of snow, and your bones solid ice, through and through and through?"

"No, I suppose not," muttered the tame pirate.

"Then give me that red tassel cap, this moment, or I shall set upon you with my stout, knobbly club."

Now the pirate felt very sorry that he had turned tame, but he did not like the look of that knobbly stick, so he gave up his red tassel cap. The snow-man put it on without a word of thanks. Then he went tramp, tramp, tramping down the hill, with the tassel bumping up and down. And the gipsy woman, and the ploughboy, and the tame pirate followed him.

At last he reached the bottom of the hill, where the village school-house stood, and there was the village schoolmaster on the doorstep, looking at the sunset. He was smoking a glowing briar pipe, and on his feet were two red velvet slippers.

"Ha! Those look warm! I must have them," said the snow-man. So he went up to the schoolmaster and said, "Give me those red slippers."

"Certainly, if you want them," said the schoolmaster. "Take them by all means. It is far too cold today to be tramping about with bare toes," and he stooped and drew off his slippers, and there he stood in some bright red socks, thick and woolly and knitted by hand.

"Ha! Those look warm! Give them to me!" said the snow-man.

"Certainly, if you want them," said the schoolmaster. "But you must come inside. I cannot take my socks off here, in the doorway. Come on to the mat."

So the snow-man stepped inside the doorway, and stood upon the mat.

"Be sharp with those socks. My feet are as cold as solid ice," he grumbled.

"I am sorry to hear that," said the schoolmaster. "But I have a warm red blanket airing over the stove. Come in, sir. Sit on that chair by the fire, sir. Put your cold feet upon this snug red footstool, and let me wrap this red blanket around your legs."

So the snow-man came into the school-house, and sat upon a chair by the glowing fire, and put his feet upon the red footstool, and the schoolmaster wrapped the red blanket round and round and round his legs. (And all this while the gipsy woman, and the ploughboy, and the tame pirate were peering in at the window).

"Are you feeling warmer?" asked the schoolmaster.

"No. I am as cold as an iceberg."

"Come closer to the fire."

So the schoolmaster pushed the chair closer to the fire, but the snow-man gave him not one word of thanks.

The Snow-man

"Are you feeling warmer now?"

"No. I am as cold as a stone. My feet feel like icy water."

"Move closer to the fire," said the schoolmaster, and he pushed the chair right against the kerb. "There! Are you warmer now?"

"No, no, no! I am colder than ever. I cannot feel my feet at all. I cannot feel my legs at all. I cannot feel my back at all."

Then the schoolmaster pushed the chair quite close up against the stove. "Are you warmer now?" he said.

But there was no answer, except a slithery sliding sound, and the drip, drip, drip of black snow-water.

"Dear me!" whispered the snow-man, in a gurgling kind of voice. "I have dropped my stout, knobbly club. My red slippers are floating into the ashpan. My mittens are swimming in a little river on the floor. My shawl is gone. My red tassel cap is slipping—slipping away. My head is going—going——"

Splosh! Splash! Gurgle!

"That's the end of him," said the schoolmaster, and he went to fetch the mop.

Then the gipsy woman, and the ploughboy and the tame pirate came in and picked up their things, and wrung them out, and dried them at the stove, and the schoolmaster put his red slippers on the hearth, and hung the red blanket over the back of the chair.

Then he picked up the stout, knobbly club and gave the fire a poke.

The Story of the Little Red Engine

——————————————*——————————————

Once upon a time there was a Little Red Engine. It lived in a big shed beside the station of Taddlecombe Junction, and every day at seven o'clock it came out of its shed to go on its journey.

As it left the station it would give a loud whistle, and that meant "Good-bye! Good-bye! It's seven o'clock, it's time to go! Good-bye! Good-bye!" and away it would go—dig-a-dig dig, dig-a-dig dig, dig-a-dig dig, all the way to Dodge, Mazy, Callington Humble, Never Over, Soke, Seven Sisters, Dumble, and home.

Now first it would pass by the Jubilee cottages and old Mrs. Ransom's little dog Hurry would come running out every morning and "Bow wow wow" he would cry; "Good morning, Little Red Engine."

And the Little Red Engine would give a whistle, WHOO-EOO, "Good morning, little dog Hurry," and on it would go with a dig-a-dig dig.

And then it would pass old Gregory's farm yard and all the ducks on the pond would cry "Quack, Quack, Quack! Good morning, Little Red Engine!"

And the Little Red Engine would give a whistle, WHOO-EOO, "Good morning, Good morning" and on it would go with a dig-a-dig dig. And then it would go by Callington Manor, and the Baronet's donkey would cry, "EE-AW! EE-AW! Good morning, Little Red Engine!": and the Little Red Engine would reply, WHOOEOO, "Good morning, Neddy," and would hurry along with a dig-a-dig dig.

And when it ran through Seldom Spinney the gamekeeper's cat who had only one eye would jump through the wire and cry "Miaow, Miaow! Good morning, Little Red Engine!"

And the Little Red Engine would say WHOOEOO, "Good morning to you," and on it would go with a dig-a-dig dig.

At Merrymans Rising the Little Red Engine would change its tune, and instead of dig-a-dig dig it would go chuffa chuffa chuffa chuff, chuffa chuffa chuffa chuff, while the sheep who grazed on the hillside would stop their eating and would all turn towards it and cry "Baa Baa, Good morning, Little Red Engine!"

The Little Red Engine would say nothing till it got to the top and then it would let out SUCH a whistle WHOOEOOEOO, "I've done it, I've done it, Good morning, Good-bye," and down the other side it would go dig-a-dig dig as fast as you please.

And last of all at Noman's Puddle the frogs, when they heard it coming, would poke their heads out of the marshes and sing REK KEK KEK KEX, REK KEK KEK KEX as loud as they could, "Good morning, Little Red Engine." And the Little Red Engine would whistle WHOOEOO, "Thank you very much." But it didn't really think the frogs had very nice voices.

And besides all this at each one of the ten level-crossings there was always the chance of a car. And the cars would go UUR UUR UUUR as cars will; "Hurry up and let me through." And the Little Red Engine would hurry up and the cars would toot "Thank you," and the Little Red Engine would whistle WHOOEOO and on it would go with a dig-a-dig dig.

But now one morning whatever was this? At seven o'clock

no Little Red Engine! Mrs. Ransom's Hurry barked "Bow WOW WOW. It's never been late before!"

Farmer Gregory's ducks went "QUACK QUACK QUACK, Whatever can have happened?"

The Baronet's donkey cried "EE-AW EE-AW I'd never have thought it!"

The gamekeeper's cat said "Miaow, Miaow, there's no knowing these days."

And the sheep on the hillside said "BAA BAA. Things are not what they were," and as for the frogs on Noman's Puddle, they made such a racket and a croaking that you couldn't distinguish a word they said; whilst the cars went whizzing over the crossings surprised that no-one stopped them.

And what had happened to the Little Red Engine? The Little Red Engine was ill!

At half past six its driver had come and had cleaned it and polished it and stoked it and got up steam but when he took the brakes off, SHHHHH sighed the Little Red Engine and did not move. The driver tried again. Chuffa Chuffa SHHHHHHH. The Little Red Engine could not go! They ran for the mechanic and told him what had happened.

"The Little Red Engine is ill, can you come and make it better?"

The mechanic came to the shed and looked at the Little Red Engine. He looked at it inside and he looked at it outside. He looked very wise. Off he went and came back with a can. "Here is the medicine to make it better. Twice a day and don't forget."

And what do you think the medicine was called? OIL!

The driver took the medicine and gave it to the Little Red Engine and no sooner did it taste it than Dig-a-dig dig, Dig-a-dig dig, they could hardly keep it on the lines! "We are late this morning. Make up for lost time," and away it went dig-a-dig dig, dig-a-dig dig, dig-a-dig dig faster than ever before.

The Story of the Little Red Engine

As it passed the cottages, "WOOF, WOOF WOOF, whatever was the matter?" "Sorry to be late, sorry to be late," and the Little Red Engine was gone.

It rushed by the duck pond "QUACK QUACK QUACK QUACK. You've come at last!"

"Sorry to be late, sorry to be late," and the Little Red Engine was gone! The Baronet's donkey cried "EE-AW EE-AW, I thought you were shirking." "Sorry to be late, sorry to be late," and there it was climbing Merrymans Rising without ever a pause to change its tune. "BAA BAA BAA, you can't keep it up, you can't keep it up."

But the Little Red Engine was down the other side before the sheep had even stopped speaking. And when the frogs saw it coming they waved their legs in the air: "Here comes old lightning! Here comes the Flying Scotsman! REK KEK KEK KEX, REK KEK KEK KEX."

And as for the cars at the crossings they had no time to say "Hurry". The Little Red Engine was by them before ever they had uttered a toot. And there it was home in the shed not one minute later than usual!

"You certainly are SOME engine," said its driver patting it proudly, and he gave it some medicine, and the Little Red Engine sighed a gentle little whistle WHOOEOO and went happily to sleep.

The Gingerbread Boy

————————————————*————————————————

In a little old house once upon a time there lived a little old man and a little old woman. They had no little boys or girls of their own and they felt rather lonely. So one fine day the little old woman made a little Gingerbread Boy. She made him a jacket out of chocolate, with raisins for buttons. She put two black juicy currants in his face for eyes and two wavy lines of bright pink sugar for his mouth. She put a cap of striped sugar-candy on his head and made his trousers out of brown marzipan. When she had baked him in the oven she took him out and put on his feet some shiny shoes made of black liquorice.

When he was all finished she stood him on the table and said happily, "Now I have a little boy of my own."

But the Gingerbread Boy jumped off the table and ran out through the kitchen doorway down the busy street. The little old man and the little old woman ran after him as fast as they could but the Gingerbread Boy laughed and shouted:

> *"Run, run as fast as you can*
> *You can't catch me*
> *I'm the Gingerbread Man!"*

And they couldn't catch him.

The Gingerbread Boy ran on and on until he passed a cow grazing in the field. "Stop, stop, little Gingerbread Boy," called the cow, "I want to eat you."

The Gingerbread Boy

The little Gingerbread Boy laughed and said:

> *"I have run away from*
> *A little old woman*
> *And a little old man*
> *And I can run away from you, can't I?"*

And as the cow began to chase him the Gingerbread Boy looked over his shoulder and cried:

> *"Run, run as fast as you can*
> *You can't catch me*
> *I'm the Gingerbread Man."*

The cow ran faster and faster but couldn't catch him.

On ran the Gingerbread Man further and further until he came to a horse munching hay by the roadside.

"Stop, stop, little Gingerbread Boy," said the horse, "I want to eat you. You'd make a nice mouthful."

But the little Gingerbread Boy laughed and shouted:

The Gingerbread Boy

"I have run away from
A little old woman
And a little old man
And a cow —
And I can run away from you, can't I"

And as the horse chased him, he looked back over his shoulder and cried:

"Run, run as fast as you can
You can't catch me, I'm the Gingerbread Man!"

The horse galloped faster and faster but couldn't catch him.

On and on ran the Gingerbread Boy until he came to a barn where lots of people were threshing grain. They tried to stop him as he passed and cried out:

"Wait, wait little Gingerbread Boy. You look very appetizing. We want to eat you."

But the little Gingerbread Boy only laughed, and shouted as he looked back over his shoulder:

"I have run away from
A little old woman
And a little old man
And a cow,
And a horse,
And I can run away from you, can't I?"

And when he was well past them he shouted:

"Run, run as fast as you can,
You can't catch me, I'm the Gingerbread Man!"

And though the threshers ran faster and faster they still couldn't catch him.

And now the Gingerbread Boy came running through a big

The Gingerbread Boy

field where lots of people were mowing grass. As soon as they caught sight of him they stopped mowing and cried:

"Stop! stop! Gingerbread Boy, we want to eat you." This only made the Gingerbread Boy run harder than ever and as he was leaving the field he called back:

> *"I have run away from*
> *A little old woman*
> *And a little old man*
> *And a cow,*
> *And a horse,*
> *And a barn full of threshers,*
> *And I can run away from you, can't I?"*

And with a last look over his shoulder he shouted:

> *"Run, run as fast as you can*
> *You can't catch me, I'm the Gingerbread Man!"*

And the mowers couldn't catch him.

The little Gingerbread Boy went running on and on and on. By this time he was sure that nobody could ever catch him. Just then he saw a fox trotting across a field towards him. The Gingerbread Boy shouted: "Hey Mr. Fox, you can't catch me, can you? I have run away from—

> *A little old woman*
> *And a little old man*
> *And a cow*
> *And a horse*
> *And a barn full of threshers*
> *And a field full of mowers*
> *And I can run away from you, can't I?*
> *Run! run! as fast as you can!*
> *You can't catch me, I'm the Gingerbread Man."*

The Gingerbread Boy

Mr. Fox was very sly. He called out: "I don't want to catch you."

Just then, the Gingerbread Boy came to a river but he had to stop because he couldn't swim. But he had to keep running because the cow and the horse and the people were still after him.

"Would you like to jump on my tail?" said Mr. Fox, "and I will take you across."

So the Gingerbread Boy jumped on Mr. Fox's tail and Mr. Fox began to swim across the river. After a little while Mr. Fox said:

"You are not very comfy on my tail, Gingerbread Boy, just move on to my back."

And the Gingerbread Boy moved on to Mr. Fox's back.

After they had gone a little further Mr. Fox said, "I'm afraid you are getting wet on my back, Gingerbread Boy. Will you move on to my shoulder?"

And the little Gingerbread Boy jumped on to Mr. Fox's shoulder.

But as they were getting near the other bank Mr. Fox said:

"I'm afraid my shoulder is sinking. Could you just hop on to my nose till we get to the other side?"

And the little Gingerbread Boy jumped on to Mr. Fox's nose.

The moment Mr. Fox reached the river-bank he tossed back his head and lo! the Gingerbread Boy was in Mr. Fox's jaws— SNAP! and that was the end of the Gingerbread Boy.

Oeyvind and His Goat

————————————————*————————————————

Once upon a time there was a little boy and his name was Oeyvind. He lived with his father and mother in a little house beside a hill. Fir and birch trees stood on the hillside, and the wild cherry let its blossoms fall on the roof of the house in the springtime.

Oeyvind had a goat. When he was not playing with it, he kept it up on the flat roof of the little house, so that it could not run away.

One day, while Oeyvind was in the house, the goat looked up to the top of the hill, and he thought, "I should like to go up there." Then he jumped over to the hillside, and climbed far up the hill to a place where he had never been before.

When Oeyvind came out of the house, he looked up to the roof, and his goat was not there. He looked all about, but he could not see it anywhere. He grew very warm for he thought his goat was lost.

"Here, killy-killy-killy-goat," he called.

He heard the goat call to him from the top of the hill. "Bay-a-a-a," it called.

The goat was looking down at Oeyvind with its head on one side. A little girl was kneeling beside it with her arms around its neck.

"Is he your goat?" said the little girl.

Oeyvind and His Goat

Oeyvind put his hands into his pockets, and said, "Who are you?"

"I am Marit," said the little girl, "mother's baby, father's mouse, little fairy in the house; four years old in autumn, two days after the first frost night, I am."

"Are you?" said Oeyvind.

"Yes. Is he your goat, and will you give him to me?" said Marit.

"He is my goat, and I will not give him to anybody," said Oeyvind.

"If I give you a butter-cake, will you give him to me?" said Marit.

Oeyvind and His Goat

Now, Oeyvind had eaten a butter-cake once; it was when his grandfather had come to see them, and he had never tasted anything so good.

"Let me see the butter-cake," he said.

"Here it is," said Marit.

She took a butter-cake out of her pocket, and threw it down to Oeyvind. It fell on the ground at his feet.

"Oh, it has all gone to pieces!" he said.

He picked up every piece of it. He tasted the smallest piece. It was so good that he tasted another piece, and another, and another; and before he thought what he was doing, he had eaten the whole cake.

"Now the goat is mine," said Marit.

"Oh no, can't you wait a bit?" said Oeyvind.

"No, no, you have eaten the cake, and the goat is mine," she said. And she put her arms around the goat's neck again. She tried to drag it away. It would not go, but stretched its neck and looked down at Oeyvind.

"Bay-a-a-a," it said.

Marit caught hold of its fleece, and pulled it along.

"Come, Goatie dear," she said, "you shall come indoors and eat from mother's pretty dish."

As she dragged the goat away, she sang a little song to it about her pets at home.

> *"Come, goat, to your sire,*
> *Come, calf from the byre;*
> *Come, pussy that mews,*
> *In your snowy-white shoes;*
> *Come, ducklings so yellow,*
> *Come, chickens so small,*
> *Each soft, little fellow,*
> *That can't run at all;*

35

Oeyvind and His Goat

Come, sweet doves of mine,
With your feathers so fine."

Now the goat was gone.

Oeyvind's mother came from the spring with fresh water, and she saw Oeyvind seated on the ground. She saw that he was crying.

"What is the matter? Why are you crying?" she asked.

"The goat, the goat!" That was all that Oeyvind could say.

His mother looked up to the roof. "Where is the goat?" she said.

"Oh, it will never come back," said Oeyvind.

"Has the fox taken it?" asked his mother.

"I wish it had been the fox," said Oeyvind. "I sold it for a butter-cake."

"Oeyvind, what do you suppose the little goat thinks of you for selling it for a butter-cake?" said his mother.

Then she went into the house with the spring water, and Oeyvind lay on the ground with his face to the grass, and cried as though he would never stop crying.

After a while he fell asleep, and while he was asleep he had a dream. He dreamt that he saw his goat up on a great white cloud.

The goat said, "Bay-a-a-a."

He wanted to come down to Oeyvind, but Oeyvind could not go up there to bring him down.

Just then something wet poked right into Oeyvind's ear. He sat up.

"Bay-a-a-a," said a voice, and there was the goat!

"Oh, you've come back! You've come back!" said Oeyvind.

He sprang to his feet, took the goat by the forelegs, and danced with it like a brother. He was taking it right in to his mother, when he saw little Marit standing there.

36

Oeyvind and His Goat

"Oh, it's you who have come with him," said Oeyvind.

"Yes, I was not allowed to keep him," said Marit.

She put her arms round the goat's neck, and cried as though her heart would break. Oeyvind looked away.

"I think you had better keep the goat," he said.

"Well, Marit," said a voice from the top of the hill.

So Marit remembered what she must do. She stood up and held her hand out to Oeyvind.

"Forgive me," she said.

Then she ran up the hill without looking back.

Oeyvind had his goat again. But he was not as happy with it as he had been before.

But the next day, and nearly every day after that, Marit came down the hill and played with Oeyvind and his goat, and then Oeyvind and Marit and the goat were all happy.

The Frog Prince

---*---

Many years ago there lived a King and Queen who had an only daughter. She was very beautiful and loved playing with her friends in the royal park, which was full of splendid trees and sparkling fountains.

One day she took her friends out to play a game with her favourite golden ball. Once the lovely golden ball was just about to drop into the Princess's hands when suddenly the sun got in her eyes. The ball dropped to her feet and rolled swiftly into a well nearby. The Princess ran forward and bent over the well, heartbroken to see her golden ball disappear into the dark green waters. She began to weep and when her friends tried to cheer her up she sent them away and just sat there alone, all sad and tear-stained.

Suddenly she heard a little croaking voice saying:

"What is the matter, little princess? Why is so beautiful a girl so sad?"

"Oh, froggie," she replied. "I am crying because my golden ball has fallen into the well."

"Never mind," said the frog, "I can easily dive down and fetch it up again."

"Can you really?" said the Princess. "Please do. I shall give you anything you wish to have, if you bring me back my golden ball! Even my golden crown!"

The Frog Prince

"I do not want your crown," replied the frog gravely. "All I want is to sit by you and eat at your table, drink from your cup and sleep in your bed."

"Oh!" exclaimed the Princess, rather taken aback. "Very well then, if that is what you want. Only do hurry, please, and fetch back my golden ball."

The frog disappeared and was back in a moment with the golden ball balanced on his head. He tossed it into the Princess's hands.

"Thank you, Frog," she said breathlessly and was off in a flash, making her way back to the palace.

"Wait, wait for me," cried the frog, hopping on to the bank. But she was gone.

Next evening the King, the Queen and the Princess were sitting at the royal table enjoying their dinner when they heard a strange voice from behind the door saying:

The Frog Prince

"Royal Princess, let me in. Remember your promise yesterday at the well."

The Princess ran hastily to the door to make sure it was really
the frog—for she could hardly believe her ears. When she saw
the frog, all dripping on the step, she quickly shut the door
again and ran back rather pale to the table.

"What is the matter, child?" asked the King. "Is there a
giant at the door?"

"No, dear father," she answered. "It is a frog who fetched
my golden ball for me yesterday when it fell into the well. And
I promised, in return, that he could come and eat at my table
and sleep in my bed." And she burst into tears.

"My dear child," said the King gently, "if that is what you
promised that is what you must do. Go and invite him in."

The Princess slowly went and opened the door. The frog
hopped in, followed her to her chair and said: "Please lift me
up beside you."

The poor Princess looked very ill at ease and the King said
sympathetically: "Come along, dear, help the Frog up," and
she did.

Then the frog said:

"Please bring your plate and put it a little nearer so that we
can eat together." And this the Princess did too, though, if the
truth were to be told, she didn't feel very hungry any more.

When the meal was over the frog said:

"I feel rather tired now. Will you please take me up to your
bedroom so that I can go to sleep in your silken bed."

The Princess shuddered slightly and hung her head. So the
King, her father, said very softly:

"Come along, dear, keep your promise and do as Frog asks."

So she gingerly picked the frog up 'twixt finger and thumb
and went upstairs on the verge of tears. She put him on a chair
in her bedroom but did not take him into bed with her.

The Frog Prince

"Oh, please," said the frog, "do please take me into your bed. I want to sleep."

The Princess stretched over, picked him up and laid him at the foot of her bed. Then she burst into sobs, buried her face in the pillow and finally fell into a deep sleep.

She awoke in the morning to bright sunshine and who should she see sitting at the foot of her bed but a handsome young Prince dressed in the most beautiful robes. She rubbed her eyes and thought she must be dreaming. Then the Prince told her how he had been changed into a frog by a wicked witch and that only a beautiful young Princess could break the spell. This had now been done. The Princess felt very grateful that her father, the wise King, had made her keep her promise.

So they became great friends and often played with the golden ball in the royal park. But it never again fell into the well.

And when the Princess was grown up into a young lady they got married and lived happily ever after.

Teeny Tiny

———————————————————*———————————————————

Along time ago there lived a teeny tiny woman who lived all by herself in a teeny tiny house in a teeny tiny village. One evening this teeny tiny woman said to her teeny tiny self, "I think I shall take a teeny tiny walk before having my teeny tiny supper." So off she went but she had gone only a teeny tiny way when she came to a teeny tiny gate and this teeny tiny gate opened on to a teeny tiny field. So through this teeny tiny gate the teeny tiny woman went and walked along the teeny tiny hedge of the teeny tiny field. After a teeny tiny while her teeny tiny glance fell upon a teeny tiny bone lying in the teeny tiny field.

"Ah!" she thought to her teeny tiny self, "this teeny tiny bone will be just the very thing for my teeny tiny supper."

So the teeny tiny woman bent down, picked up the teeny tiny bone and put it into the teeny tiny pocket of her teeny tiny coat. Then she walked back to the teeny tiny gate and returned to her teeny tiny house.

She felt a teeny tiny bit tired when she got to her teeny tiny house so instead of making her teeny tiny supper she put the teeny tiny bone into her teeny tiny cupboard and went straight off to her teeny tiny bed.

After a teeny tiny sleep in her teeny tiny bed she woke up because she thought she could hear a teeny tiny voice coming

Teeny Tiny

straight from the teeny tiny cupboard. And the teeny tiny voice kept repeating:

> *"Give me my bone!*
> *Give me my bone!*
> *Give me my bone!"*

The teeny tiny woman was just a teeny tiny bit frightened by this teeny tiny voice so she buried her teeny tiny head under the teeny tiny bedclothes and fell asleep again.

But after a teeny tiny while she was awakened once more by the teeny tiny voice crying out:

> *"Give me my bone!*
> *Give me my bone!*
> *Give me my bone!"*

And this time the teeny tiny voice seemed a teeny tiny bit louder than before.

And this made the teeny tiny woman just a teeny tiny bit more frightened, so down went her teeny tiny head once more under the teeny tiny bedclothes. This time she slept for a teeny

tiny bit longer, but when she awoke again the teeny tiny voice
had become a teeny tiny bit louder than before and cried out:

"Give me my bone!
Give me my bone!
Give me my bone!"

This time the teeny tiny woman poked her teeny tiny head
out from under the teeny tiny bedclothes and said in her loudest
teeny tiny voice:
"TAKE IT."

The Three Brothers

———————————*———————————

There once lived an old man who had three sons. He was very fond of them for they were all excellent lads. The old man didn't have much money but he did have a most comfortable house and he could not make up his mind which son to leave his house to.

"They have all been such good sons to me," he thought to himself. "I'm afraid I shall have to sell the house and share out the money I get for it among the three of them."

So he called his sons together and told them of his plan.

"Father," they said, "we know you want to be fair to us but we really don't want you to sell our comfortable house. Your grandfather and father before you, with their families, all lived in it; it is a very nice house and we all love it. Please do not sell it."

The father smiled. "I really am glad you think that way, my boys," he said. "Of course, I would rather *not* sell the house. But how else can I leave you each an equal share of what I have?"

"Listen, Father," said the eldest son, who was a very thoughtful young man. "Let all three of us go out into the world for one year to learn a trade—whichever trade we like best. And when we come back you must decide which one of us has learnt his job best. And to him you will leave the house. In that way this splendid house will not go out of the family."

The Three Brothers

The other two sons said, "Yes! Yes! An excellent idea!" So the father agreed to let them go, though he was truly sorry to be without them for a whole year.

Now what trade do you think they chose? The eldest said: "I am going to learn to be a blacksmith. I love attending to horses, and, besides, it will make my muscles very strong."

The second son said: "I have always wanted to be a barber. I can handle a razor well. That's the trade for me."

"And I," said the third, "I am going to learn to be a fencing master. I am light and nimble on my feet and I have a good eye. I think I shall make a first-rate fencing-master."

So one fine morning—it was the first of June—the three lads said goodbye to their father and set off on their separate ways. They were all going to be back by eight o'clock in the morning on the first of June the following year.

Well, the year went by slowly for the poor father, for he was lonely without his sons, but it passed very quickly for the boys. They were so busy learning their trades with their teachers that they did not notice the time passing. By about March, however, they had all finished learning their trade and each received a certificate of excellence from his master.

The eldest son was such an expert blacksmith that even the King heard about him and hired him to shoe the royal horses.

The second son, too, turned out to be a first-class barber and the smartest people came to him to have their hair and beards trimmed.

The third son found things somewhat harder, for the land was full of fine fencers and it was quite a time before his fame had spread. But he was never discouraged. He was really determined to be the best fencer, not only in the land, but in the whole world.

At last on the first of June at eight o'clock in the morning, they arrived at their father's house and he gave them a tremendous welcome. He had missed them very much.

But now the question was: how was he to find out which one had learnt his trade best? The sons didn't argue about it but each secretly thought to himself that *he* would get the house.

They all went out for a walk over the fields to think the matter over. Suddenly a little rabbit came sprinting towards them. The barber took out his mug and soap, whipped up a foaming lather and, as the rabbit was actually rushing past them, he lathered the bunny's chin and shaved it nice and clean. He did it so fast that the rabbit barely noticed.

His father was amazed. "This boy will surely have the house," he thought. "There can't be a faster barber in the whole land."

Just then a gnat came buzzing close by, flying just above their heads. The blacksmith got his tools together and in a jiffy had fitted it with tiny golden horseshoes, each shoe carefully secured with tiny golden pins that didn't hurt. He did this all the while the gnat was actually flying!

"Goodness me!" thought the father, "he's even better than his brother. I suppose I shall have to leave the house to him."

Just then it started to rain, slightly at first but then more and more heavily. But before a single drop had fallen on his head the third son had drawn his sword and swung it this way and that, and in all directions above his head, to beat each droplet away from him. Fast as the rain fell, his gleaming sword was even faster. Thick and fast it poured down, drenching all the others, but the youngest son remained absolutely dry. He flashed his sword this way and that above him, never getting tired, and he remained as dry as though he were sitting at home.

The father was absolutely amazed. "Truly remarkable!

Truly wonderful!" he said. "To you I must leave the house. Your brothers have certainly mastered their trade but you are a supreme master."

The other two brothers thoroughly agreed with their father and felt very proud of their clever young brother.

But although he won the house for himself he did not send the others away. He shared it with them and they all lived there in peace and friendship for the rest of their days.

The Elves and the Shoemaker

———————————————*———————————————

There once lived a very hard-working shoemaker and his wife. He was honest and obliging and always had his customer's shoes ready in good time. But for all that fewer and fewer people came to him to buy their shoes or to have them repaired. So in time he became very poor and soon only had just enough leather to make one single pair of shoes. One night, feeling very sad, he cut out the leather ready for stitching the shoes the next morning. Then he said his prayers and went to bed.

When he got up early next morning he was surprised to see the pair of shoes standing all ready stitched and finished on his work table. He looked for the leather that he had cut out the night before but it was nowhere to be found.

"Hey, dear," he called to his wife, "who has brought this new pair of shoes on the table here, and what has happened to the leather I cut out last night?"

But his wife was as puzzled as he was.

Just then a customer came in to buy a pair of shoes. The ones on the table happened to be exactly his size and they fitted him most comfortably. Besides, they were so excellently made and stitched that he gave the old shoemaker a very good price for them. And now the shoemaker was able to buy enough leather to make two more pairs of shoes.

The Elves and the Shoemaker

He cut out the leather that night ready for the next morning, laid the pieces on his work table, said his prayers and went to bed.

When he got up next morning he was amazed to see TWO brand new pairs of shoes on his work table, and the pieces of leather he had cut out had again vanished. Again, two very satisfied customers bought the shoes and so now he had enough money to buy leather for FOUR new pairs.

He cut out the leather in readiness to make the shoes the next morning and laid the pieces neatly on his work table. Then he said his prayers and went off to sleep.

The next morning—the same thing. There were now FOUR pairs of shoes—all finished and ready for selling, all excellently stitched and made.

And this went on happening night after night until the shoemaker and his wife became quite rich.

One night his wife said: "Supposing we sat up tonight instead of going to bed? We might see this mysterious creature who has been so kindly making these shoes for us." The shoemaker thought this was an excellent idea, so they hid behind a cupboard in the corner and began to watch.

As midnight chimed two naked little elves crept into the room, sat on the work table and began busily working on the pieces of leather that the shoemaker had prepared. They stitched, pierced and sewed, stitched, pierced and sewed, hammered and hammered very cleverly and swiftly, never stopping to rest or to even pause for breath. Their fingers moved so fast that the eyes of the shoemaker and his wife could scarcely keep pace with them. And when all the shoes were finished they jumped down from the table and disappeared.

"Well goodness gracious me!" said the shoemaker's wife. "Fancy those naked little men being so kind to us. And how nimble and clever they are! But they must feel terribly cold running about with no clothes to cover their little bodies. I must make them some shirts and jackets and trousers and stockings. And you must stitch them each a neat, solid pair of shoes.''

The shoemaker was only too pleased to agree with his wife's suggestion and they set to work right away.

By the next evening they had all the clothes and shoes ready, one set for each elf, and they placed them carefully on the table. But this time the shoemaker did not leave any cut-out leather for them. They left one small candle burning in the room and hid behind the cupboard to watch.

Promptly at midnight in rushed the naked little elves all ready to set to work. Imagine the expression on their faces when they saw what was waiting for them! No leather for stitching into shoes but, instead, two complete sets of clothes and shoes! All newly sewn. Their little faces, at first full of surprise, became wreathed in the broadest of smiles and they immediately

started to put the clothes on in great excitement, singing all the time.

Then, when they were all dressed, they hopped and danced *round* the table, *on* the table, *under* the table and at last *out through the door*.

From that time onward the shoemaker and his wife never saw the elves again but they now had enough work and money and they lived happily for the rest of their lives.

The Laughing Dragon

———————————*———————————

There was once a king who had a very loud voice, and three sons.

His voice was *very* loud. It was so loud that when he spoke every one jumped. So they called the country he ruled over by the name of Jumpy.

But one day the king spoke in a very low voice indeed. And all the people ran about and said, "The King is going to die."

He *was* going to die, and he *did* die. But before he died he called his three sons to his bedside. He gave one half of Jumpy to the eldest son; and he gave the other half to the second son. Then he said to the third, "You shall have six shillings and eightpence farthing and the small bag in my private box."

In due time the third son got his six shillings and eightpence farthing, and put it safely away into his purse.

Then he got the bag from the King's private box. It was a small bag made of kid, and was tied with a string.

The third son, whose name, by the way, was Tumpy, untied the string and looked into the bag. It had nothing in it but a very queer smell. Tumpy sniffed and then he sneezed. Then he laughed, and laughed, and he laughed again without in the least knowing what he was laughing at.

"I shall never stop laughing," he said to himself. But he did, after half an hour and two minutes exactly. Then he smiled for three minutes and a half exactly again.

After that he looked very happy; and he kept on looking so happy that people called him Happy Tumpy, or H.T. for short.

Next day H.T. set out to seek his fortune. He had tied up the bag again and put it into the very middle of his bundle.

His mother gave him some bread and a piece of cheese, two apples and a banana. Then he set out with a happy face. He whistled as he went along with his bundle on a stick over his shoulder.

After a time he was tired, and sat down on a large milestone. As he was eating an apple, a black cat came along. It rubbed its side against the large stone, and H.T. stroked its head.

Then it sniffed at the bundle that lay on the grass. Next it sneezed, and then it began to laugh. It looked so funny that H.T. began to laugh too.

"You must come with me, puss," said H.T. The cat was now smiling broadly. It looked up at H.T. and he fed it. Then they went on side by side.

By and by H.T. and the cat came to a town, and met a tall, thin man. "Hallo," he said, and H.T. said the same.

"Where are you going?" asked the man.

"To seek my fortune," said H.T.

"I would give a small fortune to the man who could make me laugh."

"Why?" said H.T.

"Because I want to be fat," said the man, "and people always say 'laugh and grow fat'."

"How much will you give?" said H.T.

"Oh, five shillings and twopence halfpenny anyhow," said the man.

H.T. put down his bundle and took out his bag. He held it near the man's face and untied the string. The man sniffed and then he sneezed. Then he laughed for half an hour and two minutes. Next he smiled for three minutes and a half.

By that time he was quite fat. So he paid H.T. five shillings and twopence halfpenny. Then he went on his way with a smile and a wave of the hand.

"That is good," said H.T. "If I go on like this I shall soon make my fortune." He tied up his bag and went on again. The black cat walked after him with a smile on its face that never came off.

After an hour the two companions came to another town. There were a lot of men in the street, but no women, or boys, or girls. The men looked much afraid. H.T. went up to one of them, "Why do you look so much afraid?" he asked politely.

"You will look afraid too, very soon," said the man. "The great dragon is coming again. It comes to the town each day, and it takes a man and a cheese. In ten minutes it will be here."

"Why don't you fight it?" asked H.T. "It is too big and fierce," said the man. "If any man could kill it he would make his fortune." "How is that?" said H.T. "Well," said the man, "the King would give him a bag of gold, and make the Princess marry him."

All at once H.T. heard a loud shout.

"The dragon is coming!" called a man who wore a butcher's apron. Then he ran into his shop, banged the door, and threw a large piece of meat out of the window. There was now nothing in the street but H.T., the cat, and the piece of meat.

H.T. did not run away, not even when he saw the huge dragon come lumbering up the street on all fours. It crept along, and turned its head this way and that. Its face had a terrible look.

Fire came out of its nose when it blew out. And three of the houses began to burn. Then it came to the meat. It sniffed and stopped to eat it. That gave H.T. time for carrying out his plan.

55

The Laughing Dragon

He took out his bag and untied the string. Then he threw it down before the dragon. On it came, blowing more fire from its nostrils. Soon the butcher's shop was burning. There was a noise like the noise from an oven when the meat is roasting.

The dragon still came on. When it got up to the bag it stopped. It sniffed. Then it sneezed so hard that two houses fell down flat. Next it began to laugh, and the noise was so loud that the church steeple fell into the street.

Of course it had stopped to laugh. It sat up on its hind legs and held its sides with its forepaws. Then it began to smile. And a dragon's smile, you must understand, is about six feet wide!

The dragon looked so jolly that H.T. did not feel afraid of it any more; not in the least. He went up to it and took one of its forepaws into his arm. The cat jumped on the dragon's head. And they all went along the street as jolly as sandboys.

A woman popped her head out of a high window. "Take the

first to the right," she said, "and the second to the left. Then you will come to the King's royal palace. You cannot miss it."

"Thank you very much," said H.T.; and he and the dragon and the cat smiled up at her. H.T. waved his hand. The dragon waved its other forepaw. And the cat waved its tail.

So they went on—down one street and then another. At last they came to a big, open, green space in which stood a big palace. It had a wall round it with four large gates in it. At each gate there was a sentry box. But not one sentry could be seen.

H.T., with his friend the dragon, came smiling up to one of the gates. Above the gate H.T. saw someone peeping over the wall. "He wears a crown," he said to the dragon, "so it must be the King." The dragon kept on smiling.

"Hallo!" cried the King. "What do *you* want?"

"Hallo!" cried H.T. "I want the bag of gold and the Princess."

"But you have not killed the dragon," said the King.

"I should think not," said H.T. "Why, he is my friend. He is my very dear friend. He will not do any harm now. Look at him."

The King stood up and put his crown straight. It had fallen over one eye in his fright. The dragon went on smiling in a sleepy way. There was no fire in his nose now.

"But," said the King, "how do I know he will not begin to kill people again?"

"Well," said H.T., "we will make a big kennel for him and give him a silver chain. Each day I will give him a sniff from my empty bag. Then he will be happy all day and go to sleep every night."

"Very well," said the King. "Here is the bag of gold. You will find the Princess in the laundry. She always irons my collars. And you can have my crown as well. It is very hard and heavy. I do not want to be King any more. I only want to sit by the fire and have a pipe and play the gramophone."

So he threw his crown down from the wall. The dragon caught it on his tail and put it on H.T.'s head. Then H.T. went to the laundry and married the Princess right away.

And the dragon lived happily ever after; and so did the cat; and so did everybody else, at least until they died.

I ought to tell you that King H.T. used the bag all his life to keep the dragon laughing. He died at the age of 301 years, one month, a week, and two days.

The next day the dragon took a very hard sniff at the bag. And he laughed so much that he *died* of laughing.

So they gave the bag to the dentist. And when any one had to have a tooth out he took a sniff. Then he laughed so much that he did not feel any pain. And when the tooth was out he was happy ever after, or at least until the next time he ate too many sweets.

The Three Wishes

———————————————*———————————————

Once upon a time there lived a poor old woodcutter and his wife in a little cottage at the edge of the forest. Every day the poor man came back home tired, hungry and weary after the heavy work he had done.

"Ah," he said to his wife one evening, "if only my wishes could come true, how happy we should be!"

"What do you mean, husband?" asked the wife crossly. "You are never satisfied. We have health and strength and a cottage to live in, so why grumble?"

But the poor man was not content and he kept on thinking how nice it would be if his wishes could come true.

One morning he was just about to fell a huge tree with his axe, when a little elf appeared at his elbow from nowhere and said, "Good morning, Mr. Woodcutter, please don't cut this tree down. If you don't I will grant you any three wishes that may be made in your cottage."

The old woodcutter was so dazed he did not know what to say or do. So he muttered in confusion:

"All right, just as you say." And the elf disappeared into thin air and was never seen again.

The old woodcutter rushed home to his wife and in great excitement told her what had happened.

But instead of being delighted as he expected she would be, she was more cross than ever and said:

"Silly husband, fancy listening to an elf. We need that firewood. Don't let it happen again." And she went on scolding the poor woodcutter all day long until suppertime came. And she was still cross even then and would not give him any supper.

"Ah!" said the old man as he sat by the empty table almost famished, "I wish I had a good string of juicy sausages. I'm fair starvin'."

No sooner were the words out of his mouth than there was a great clatter, clatter, clatter, the door flew open, and a long string of juicy red sausages came to land on the table in front of him.

Was his wife surprised? Not at all! She became crosser than ever.

"What a silly thing to wish!" she cried. "I only wish they had landed at the end of your nose." No sooner had she said these words than—SWISH, SWIZZLE and YAKKITY-DOZE and the sausages hung at the end of his nose.

"Goodness gracious me," cried the wife, "I didn't know that my wishes would come true as well."

"Yes, yes!" said her poor husband. "Any wishes that are made in this cottage. That's what the elf said."

Well, he started to pull at the sausages. He pulled and pulled with all his might and main, but they still stuck to his nose.

"Help me, good wife," he pleaded. "Please help me!"

His wife realized he looked rather silly like that so she began to tug as well. They both tugged and tugged until they nearly pulled the poor woodcutter's nose off. But the sausages stuck fast and refused to budge.

"What will the neighbours think?" thought the wife.

"Well, I've got one wish left," said the husband, "I wish these sausages were off and gone."

No sooner had he said these words than—SWISH, SIZZLE and YAKKITY-BON and the juicy sausages were off and gone!

The Three Wishes

So now all three wishes had been made.

And so the woodcutter and his wife settled down once more to their usual life at the cottage but from now on the husband remained content with his work and never again spent his time dreaming of wishes coming true.

Mr. Buffin and Harold Trotter

————————————————*————————————————

Harold Trotter was the name of Mr. Buffin's pig. He was called Harold after Mr. Buffin's uncle, General Sir Harold Buffin, K.C.B., and Trotter because that happened to be his name. Mr. Buffin's uncle, a very famous man, had been Governor of several places where it was always very hot and very wet, and Mr. Buffin hoped that Harold Trotter would live up to the name of Harold and become a very famous pig.

But Harold Trotter showed very little promise of becoming famous. He was in fact a simple-minded pig, and it meant nothing to him what Mr. Buffin's uncle had done or where he had been. Harold Trotter had but three interests in life, and they were eating, sleeping and having his back scratched. These he thought were the chief things in life and the only things worth thinking about.

Sometimes when Mr. Buffin was walking in the neighbourhood of Harold Trotter's sty, he would take a bamboo cane from the potting-shed in the garden and scratch Harold Trotter's back with it. Harold Trotter would remain quite still enjoying the lovely shivers that ran up and down his spine. Every now and then he would express his pleasure in little grunts and squeaks of delight, and when Mr. Buffin stopped scratching he would give a louder squeak, which was his way of asking for more.

Mr. Buffin and Harold Trotter

The sty was Harold Trotter's home, but as the door was always left open he was free to wander where he pleased. Mr. Buffin left the door open on purpose because he thought that life in a pigsty must be a very boring sort of life, and that if Harold Trotter was free to wander where he pleased it might help him to become a famous pig. When Harold Trotter was outside the sty he would wander round the garden scratching his back against all sorts of things. Some things made better scratching things than others, and Harold Trotter had several favourite scratching places.

One favourite scratching place was the row of young trees that Mr. Buffin had planted beside the drive that led up to the house. The stems of the trees were springy, and that made them really good scratchers. Other favourite places were a garden seat, a drainpipe and a water-butt into which ran the rain-water from the roof.

· It was this habit of looking for scratching places that got Harold Trotter into very serious trouble, such serious trouble that it was nearly the end of him. Even now, when the trouble is all over, Harold Trotter hates to think about how serious it was.

It happened like this. One day when Mr. Buffin was walking round his garden, thinking of nothing in particular but having a good look at everything, he noticed that a white climbing rose, called White Knite, which grew up the side of his house, wanted tying back to the wall.

"Dear me," said Mr. Buffin, when he saw the roses swaying to and fro on the end of their branches, "that means getting a ladder."

Mr. Buffin did not like ladders; that is to say he had nothing against ladders in themselves, but he disliked fetching them, carrying them and climbing up them. All of which sounds as though he had a great many ladders; actually he had only one.

Mr. Buffin and Harold Trotter

And yet another reason for disliking them: he always felt giddy when he got to the top of a ladder. Like many other people, Mr. Buffin could not look down from a height. It made him think about what it would be like to fall through the air and to go on falling until the bottom was reached. And that made him feel giddy.

However, Mr. Buffin tried to forget all about giddiness and heights, and went round to the potting-shed, took the ladder off the hooks on which it hung and carried it round to the front of the house. He then placed the ladder against the wall behind the climbing rose.

"There," said Mr. Buffin, who was trying hard to think of some excuse for not going up the ladder. But as he could think of none, he took his courage in both hands and said very quickly, "One, two, three, up!"

On the word "up", Mr. Buffin said "One, two, three, up!" again because, although his courage was in both hands, his mind was not quite made up. It took a little time to make up his mind, and then after one more "One, two, three, up!" Mr. Buffin started to climb. He climbed to the top. It was not as bad as he had thought, and after a short time he had tied most of the roses back against the wall.

It was while he was tying up the last of the roses that Harold Trotter came round the corner and saw the bottom of the ladder.

"Hullo, a brand-new scratching place," he said to himself. And going as fast as he could, which was not very fast because he was so fat, he got behind the ladder and began to rub himself against it. It was delicious.

Mr. Buffin felt the ladder moving.

"I knew I should feel giddy if I stayed up here," said Mr. Buffin, clutching a rung of the ladder and shutting his eyes.

By now Harold Trotter was rubbing as hard as he could.

65

Mr. Buffin and Harold Trotter

Never had he had a better scratch. It was superb. The more he shoved and the more he pushed, the better it was.

But Harold Trotter went just a little too far. He rubbed and pushed and shoved and scratched so hard that he turned the ladder right over.

"Help, help!" shouted Mr. Buffin, who had lost his grip and his balance, and was falling head foremost to the ground. But nothing could help Mr. Buffin now. Even if there had been someone there, he could have done nothing to save him. Mr. Buffin was heading straight for the ground, and, sure enough, he hit it. Or, as Mr. Buffin was inclined to think, it hit him. Mr. Buffin saw a great many stars of different sizes and colours, and several things that looked like plates moving from left to right.

When Mr. Buffin opened his eyes the stars and plates had gone and he saw Harold Trotter.

"So that was you, was it?" said Mr. Buffin. "You wait until I've looked after myself, and then I'll attend to you."

Mr. Buffin was not only hurt, he was very angry, and he was all the more angry because besides being hurt he had been frightened. And there is nothing that is more likely to make one angry than being frightened.

Mr. Buffin went into the house and put a bandage round his head. He wound several more yards of bandage than were strictly necessary, but as he had been hurt he meant to look it. And then he put some ointment round his eye, which was beginning to go black and blue and yellow. Altogether Mr. Buffin felt very sorry for himself, and still more so when he looked in the glass, which he kept on doing throughout the day.

When he began to think about Harold Trotter, Mr. Buffin thought long and seriously. Gradually Mr. Buffin arrived at his decision. He decided that there was only one thing to do and that was to take Harold Trotter to market and sell him. Mr. Buffin wanted to see no more of Harold Trotter. Mr. Buffin was angry.

Mr. Buffin and Harold Trotter

Meanwhile Harold Trotter was walking happily round the garden, scratching himself against this and against that, and having no idea at all that Mr. Buffin had made such an important decision—a decision that was to be followed by such unpleasant results.

The next morning Mr. Buffin got his car out of the garage. The car was rather an old-fashioned one. It was painted mauve and had brass lamps. Mr. Buffin did not like motor cars, and that being so he saw no point in having an expensive new car.

With Harold Trotter on the seat beside him, Mr. Buffin set out for market. Harold Trotter had no idea where he was going, and he sat on the seat with his ears pricked and thoroughly enjoyed the fresh air and the scenery.

The market was a long way off, and while the old car was puffing and panting along, Mr. Buffin began to think.

"If I sell Harold Trotter in the market," thought Mr. Buffin, "he may go to the butcher's and be killed. He may be turned into sausages. And I wouldn't like that to happen," thought Mr. Buffin, "indeed I wouldn't."

At this point of the journey the road ran through a deep, dark wood which was full of oak trees.

"I know," thought Mr. Buffin, "I'll leave Harold Trotter in this wood. He can live on the acorns and I need never be bothered with, or hurt by, him again." This struck Mr. Buffin as a very good way out of the difficulty, and so he pushed Harold Trotter out of the car, turned the car round and started for home.

Harold Trotter felt very sad and lonely, as well as deserted and hungry. He had never been alone in a big wood before, and as he watched Mr. Buffin drive away a large tear rolled down his cheek. In next to no time the car was so far away that Harold Trotter could no longer hear it. He was alone, all alone in the big dark wood. He ate some acorns.

Mr. Buffin and Harold Trotter

Harold Trotter very soon found that acorns were no good. It took him a very long time to collect enough to make a good mouthful; in fact it took him so long that he could not collect acorns fast enough to keep pace with his hunger. Harold Trotter knew that if he collected all the acorns in the wood he would still feel hungry. And in addition to this, he did not like acorns.

And so Harold Trotter made up his mind to go home. It would be a very, very long journey and would probably take him weeks, if not months, but Harold Trotter meant to go through with it. And Harold Trotter stamped each one of his feet to show himself how determined he was.

Harold Trotter started off at once. He had a good sense of direction and knew that he would not lose the way. Being a very fat pig he soon became tired and often had to sit down for rests. But as the days went by he became thinner, from having both so much exercise and so little to eat; and because he was thinner he was able to squeeze under gates and so to take short cuts.

Even so the journey took him a long time, during all of which he grew thinner and thinner, and more and more footsore. When at last he arrived at Mr. Buffin's front door, he was a very thin pig indeed. He stood on the doorstep, looking up at the green door, and he had only just enough strength to give two feeble snorts.

For many days Mr. Buffin had been worrying about Harold Trotter. Mr. Buffin's head had healed and his eye was all right, and so he was beginning to think that he had been unkind to Harold Trotter. He was beginning to wonder how Harold Trotter was getting on, whether he was finding enough to eat and whether the nights were cold. Mr. Buffin was in fact thinking of going to look for Harold Trotter when to his surprise he heard two feeble snorts.

"Can that be him?" wondered Mr. Buffin. "No, of course

it can't." But there came another two feeble snorts, and Mr. Buffin went to the door. "My goodness, it is him," cried Mr. Buffin, who was overjoyed to see Harold Trotter again.

Harold Trotter was very pleased to see Mr. Buffin, and would have wagged his tail if it had not been screwed up into such a tight twist.

Mr. Buffin took Harold Trotter into the house and fed him on all the good things he could find. Harold Trotter soon began to recover and to put on weight. In fact, he became even fatter than he had been before, so fat, indeed, that he was only a short distance off the ground. However, that did not worry Harold Trotter. A pig is never happier than when he is really fat. There are many reasons for this, and one of them is that the fatter a pig is the more room he has for scratching.

Harold Trotter went back to all his old scratching places and had a good rub, and now when the weather is fine and warm he is usually sure to find a pail of something good to eat beside Mr. Buffin's garden chair.

The Three Bears

———————————*———————————

The Bear family lived in a comfortable cottage in the woods. There was Father, a great big bear, and there was Mother, a medium-sized bear, and there was Baby, a wee little bear.

The Bear family always had porridge for breakfast. Father Bear ate his from a great big bowl, Mother Bear ate hers from a medium-sized bowl and Baby Bear ate his from a wee little bowl.

There were three comfortable chairs to sit on. Father Bear's was a great big chair, Mother Bear's was a medium-sized chair and Baby Bear just had a wee little chair.

Their beds were nice and cosy too. Father Bear's bed, as you can imagine, was a great big thing; Mother Bear just had a moderate-sized bed and Baby Bear's was a wee little bed.

Now one winter's morning, Mother Bear had made the porridge for them as usual and had poured it into the three bowls ready for breakfast. But it was so steaming hot that the Bear family decided to take a brisk walk in the woods to allow it to cool down a little.

That very same morning a little girl named Goldilocks also happened to be out taking a walk. She, too, had popped out while her mother was preparing breakfast but had wandered rather far from her home and was now feeling a little tired. She was just passing the Bears' cottage and as she glanced through the window she thought, "I must sit down for a little while to rest my weary legs." So she knocked at the door and as there was no reply she walked right in and she could smell the smell of lovely hot porridge. She was so tempted that she had a little taste of Father Bear's porridge. But that was far too hot. Then she tasted Mother Bear's porridge but that was too cool. And then she tried Baby Bear's and that was just right and she went on tasting it until she had eaten it all up.

"I simply must sit down a while," she thought. So she sat on Father Bear's great big chair, but it was terribly hard. Then she sat on Mother Bear's medium-sized chair. But she found that one was too soft. Then she sat in Baby Bear's wee little chair and that one was just right but when she plomped right into it the bottom fell out and Goldilocks found herself sitting on the floor.

Then she noticed the little stairway leading upstairs to the bedrooms. She was rather curious to see what the beds were like, so up she went. First she lay down on Father Bear's great big bed but somehow she felt it was too high for her. So then she tried Mother Bear's medium-sized bed but that was too low. So then she stretched herself out on Baby Bear's bed and that was so very comfortable that she fell asleep almost at once.

Now Goldilocks had left the spoon on Father Bear's great big bowl of porridge and when the Bear family came back from their walk, Father Bear growled out in his heavy gruff voice:

"Somebody has been eating my porridge."

Then Mother Bear looked at her bowl and said in her medium voice: "And somebody has been eating my porridge."

And Baby Bear looked at his empty bowl and cried in his wee little voice: "Somebody has been eating my porridge and has finished it all up."

Then Father Bear noticed that the cushion on his chair was

The Three Bears

not straight. "Somebody has been sitting on my chair," he growled in his great gruff voice.

And Mother Bear saw that her cushion was not straight either and she said in her medium voice: "Somebody has been sitting in my chair."

And Baby Bear cried out in his wee little voice: "Somebody has been sitting in my chair and has knocked the bottom out!"

Then the three bears all went upstairs to their bedrooms. On Father Bear's great big bed the pillow was out of place.

"Somebody has been lying on My bed!" he growled in his great gruff voice.

Mother Bear looked at her medium-sized bed and saw that one of her cushions was squashed.

"Somebody has been lying in My bed," she said in her medium voice.

Then Baby Bear looked at his wee little bed and said in his

tiny little voice: "Somebody has been lying on My bed—and IS STILL LYING ON IT."

To Goldilocks, who was sound asleep, the voices of Father Bear and Mother Bear had sounded as though she were in a dream and she did not wake up. But when she heard the high tiny voice of Baby Bear, who was standing right close to the bed, it gave her such a start that she jumped up with a jerk. And when she saw the three bears beside the bed, all staring at her, she rolled off the bed on the other side and jumped out of the window into the garden. Then she scampered like lightning through the woods, not daring to look back.

The three bears ran to the window, rather taken aback by the speed of all this, and Baby Bear said in his high tiny voice:

"She looked such a nice little girl, I do wish she had stayed to play with me!"

The Nose

———————————*———————————

There were once three poor soldiers. They had fought in many wars and now when peace was come they had no money at all and so they had to beg their food all the way home.

One dark evening they found themselves in a wood far from any town or village and so they decided to sleep in the wood for the night.

"We can't all go to sleep at the same time," said one of the soldiers. "Some wild beast may come and attack us."

So they decided to sleep two at a time while the third one stayed awake to keep watch. And when he was tired he would go to sleep and another one would keep watch. In this way each one would get his share of sleep and be in no danger.

So two of the soldiers lay down and were soon fast asleep. The third one made himself a good fire under the trees and sat down to keep watch. All of a sudden he heard a rustling among the branches and a quaint little man in a scarlet jacket appeared.

"Who are you?" asked the little man.

"I'm a poor soldier come back from the wars. I'm keeping watch over my two comrades. Come and sit down and warm yourself by the fire."

"That's most kind of you," said the little man. "Take this, my friend," he added, handing the surprised soldier a beautiful red cloak. "Whenever you put this around your shoulders you can have anything you wish for." The little man gave a low bow and disappeared among the trees.

After a while it was the second soldier's turn to keep watch and the first soldier lay down to sleep. Very soon the little man in the scarlet coat suddenly emerged from the trees once more and asked the soldier who he was.

"I and my two friends have just returned from fighting in the wars," he replied. "We are a long way from home and are very tired. So we are taking turns to sleep. Won't you join me and have a rest by this warm fire?"

The little man was delighted by the soldier's friendly manner and after warming himself by the fire he gave him a purse.

"This purse," he said as he left, "will always be full of gold, no matter how much you take out of it."

Soon came the third soldier's turn to keep watch and once more the little man appeared from somewhere behind the trees. The third soldier was also very polite and friendly to him and asked him to have a rest by the fire.

"You are very kind," said the little man. "Would you like to take this horn as a gift from me? Whenever you play upon it crowds and crowds of people will come and gather round you to dance to the beautiful music." And he disappeared among the trees.

In the morning the soldiers told one another about the little man and each one showed the others the present he had been given. They decided to use the wonderful purse and to travel all round the world with the gold that it gave. They travelled to many countries and saw lots of marvellous things but at last they grew tired of going from place to place and decided to settle down somewhere. The first soldier put the red cloak around his shoulders and wished for a fine castle. Immediately it stood before them—a tall, strong castle, with golden, gleaming turrets, surrounded by smooth, velvet lawns and gardens. There was also a large stable with fine horses and a grand coach with glass windows. They immediately took a fancy to this coach and, forgetting the castle for a moment, they decided to visit the palace of a famous King who lived not far away. The King thought they were rich princes, and made them very welcome. He introduced them to his very beautiful only daughter. But she was only beautiful on the outside. Inside she had the heart of a cruel witch. One morning the second soldier was out walking with the princess in the gardens and he showed her his wonderful purse. She immediately took a fancy to it and thought of a scheme to steal it from him. She went up to her room and made another purse that looked exactly like the soldier's purse and after dinner that evening, when the soldiers had fallen asleep after drinking rather a lot of wine, she stole the magic purse from his pocket and put her own there in its place.

The next day the soldiers returned to their castle. When the soldier opened his purse to get some gold he was astonished to find it empty. "Ah," he said suddenly, "I know what has happened. That princess was very interested in my purse. She must have stolen it from me when I was asleep and put this empty one there in its place. Oh dear! What are we to do now without any money?"

"Don't worry, my friend," said the first soldier. "I will soon get the purse back." And he flung his red cloak about his shoulders and wished himself in the royal palace. There he found the princess in her room greedily counting the pieces of gold that kept coming out of the magic purse. Suddenly she felt the soldier staring at her and in a fright she screamed: "Thieves! Thieves! Help! Thieves!"

The poor soldier was scared because lots of people came rushing into the room from all parts of the royal palace. So he ran to the window and in his hurry forgot to use his magic cloak.

The Nose

He jumped out into the garden and scampered off as fast as his legs could carry him. But it was not his lucky day for as he ran his cloak got caught in some bushes and he had to leave it behind. The princess was, of course, overjoyed, because she well knew the power of that cloak.

Our poor soldier arrived home a very sad man indeed. The third soldier cheered him up by playing a jolly tune on the horn that the little man in the scarlet coat had given him. But, of course, as soon as he started to play a great crowd of people gathered in the castle-grounds, some on foot and some on horseback.

And the first soldier said:

"Let us lead these people to the palace and make the wicked princess give back the purse and cloak."

This they did and the King, very alarmed, tried to persuade the princess to return the stolen articles.

"Oh no!" says she. "Let me see if I can beat them some other way." So she dressed herself in shabby clothes and, with a basket on her arm, set out at night, pretending that she was a poor girl with a few knick-knacks to sell, such as ribbons, safety pins and thimbles.

But in the morning, when everybody was up and wide awake, the princess began to sing an enchanting song that cast a spell over everyone. Every single person stood stock still and listened, spell-bound, to her strange song. And the three soldiers also stood perfectly still and listened. Then the princess's maid slipped into the soldier's tent where his horn was hanging and stole it away. And then the princess finished her song and all the people went away from the palace.

The three soldiers now had nothing—neither purse, nor cloak, nor horn. They sat for a long time and discussed what they should do. At last the second soldier, the one who had lost his purse, said:

"Friends, let us separate and let each one of us seek his fortune by himself." So off he went, but the other two decided to travel on together. The second soldier walked and walked until he arrived at last at that very same wood where the little man in the scarlet coat had first appeared. The soldier was very weary and lay down to sleep under a tree. When he awoke to bright sunshine the next morning he was delighted to find that the tree was laden with delicious-looking rosy apples. He was very hungry so he began eating, first one then another, then a third. Then his nose began to feel odd. He put his hand to it and—good heavens!—it was growing longer and longer and longer. By now his nose had reached the ground but it still did not stop growing. It went on and on and on till it stretched right through to the end of the wood. The poor soldier sat still in great alarm and despair.

Meanwhile his two friends, as they travelled along, suddenly stumbled against something. They could not decide what

exactly it was, so they followed it and soon realized that it must be a nose.

"Let us keep following it," said one of them, "and see to whom this marvellous, enormous nose belongs."

This they did and you can imagine their surprise when they traced it back to their old friend lying helpless under the apple-tree. They tried to lift him but in vain. They hailed a driver with his horse who was passing by. But even the horse could not carry so heavy a load. And so there they were, all three of them, very sad indeed, when up sprang from nowhere, the little man in the scarlet coat.

"Cheer up," he said with a smile, "I can soon cure your friend's trouble. Just go and pick a pear from that pear-tree over there," he said to the first soldier. Then the little man cut off a fairly large slice of pear and gave it to the poor soldier to eat. In less than no time his nose was back to its normal size.

"Now listen to me," continued the little man. "Just pick a few of these apples and put them in your pockets. Then go to the princess and get her to eat one. Tell her they are the tastiest apples in the world." And the little man disappeared among the trees.

It was decided that the soldier whose nose had been cured should dress up as a gardener's boy and take some apples to the princess as a very special gift to Her Royal Highness.

The princess was delighted to receive such a pleasant gift. The apples did look most temptingly ripe and rosy and she was soon munching away at them. She had eaten only one and a bit when her nose began growing longer and longer till it reached down to the ground and out into the royal gardens.

The King, her father, was in a dreadful state and made an announcement from the palace balcony that his daughter was suffering from a terrible disease and that anyone who could cure her would get a rich reward. So now the soldier dressed himself

The Nose

up as a very important-looking doctor. He came to the palace and said that he alone had the remedy that could cure the princess's illness.

The 'doctor' was shown into the princess's room and he asked for a plate and a knife. Then he chopped up an apple very carefully and told the princess to take a little twice a day and he would call again tomorrow. Of course, the soldier knew her nose would grow even longer by doing this, but he was determined to punish her a little. When he called the next day the princess was in a terrible state. This time the 'doctor' chopped up part of the magic pear that he had brought with him and told her to take some three times daily. When he called the next day the princess said her nose had indeed grown a wee bit smaller but it was still bigger than when the doctor had first called. The soldier thought to himself: "I can see that I must punish this wicked princess a little more before she is ready to give back what she has stolen." So he gave her another dose of chopped apple and said he would call again the next day. Tomorrow came and the princess's nose was five times longer than before.

"What on earth is the matter!" she cried. "It's getting worse and worse!"

"My dear lady," replied the soldier, "it is not my medicine that is at fault but you. I know you have stolen certain things and until you give them back your nose will not get better."

The princess was furious and said she hadn't stolen anything. "Very well," said the soldier, "as you wish. I shall report the situation to His Majesty, your father."

When the King heard the doctor's report he at once ordered the princess to give back the cloak, the purse and the horn.

So the princess sent for the doctor, gave him back all three things and begged him to return them to the three soldiers from whom she had stolen them. Once the things were safely in his hands the soldier gave her a whole pear to eat and immediately her nose became its proper size.

So the soldier wished the King and his daughter good-day, put on the cloak and was soon back with his two friends once more.

From then onwards they lived in great comfort and happiness in their castle.

Flowerbell

————————————————*————————————————

A very long time ago there lived a poor shoemaker and his wife. They had no children and their little cottage was next door to that of an old witch who had a splendid garden. The shoemaker's wife would often sit by her window and gaze longingly at the lovely flowers and vegetables next door. There was one vegetable in particular that she would stare at, it was the rampion or bell-flower. One day she said to her husband:

"Do you know, I would love to have some of that delicious rampion from the witch's garden. It would make a very tasty salad."

"But my dear," said her husband, "you know the witch would never let us have any. She is mean and cruel."

But every day afterwards the wife kept nagging her husband about the rampion, and at last she said, "I will die if you don't get me some."

So when it was very dark he climbed over the wall and jumped softly into the witch's garden. With beating heart he quickly pulled up a few rampion plants, climbed back and took them up to his wife.

She made a most wonderful salad but no sooner had she finished eating it than she turned to her husband and said:

"Now that I have tasted it, I must have some more. If I don't, I know I shall die."

Flowerbell

So the next night her poor husband had to climb over the wall once more. He was just about to pick a nice fat rampion when he saw the horrible figure of the witch towering over him.

"Oh, please don't be angry with me!" cried the poor man in terror. "I am not a thief really. But my wife had such a longing for your delicious rampions that she said she would die if she did not have some to eat."

The witch gave a horrible smile.

"Do not fear, little man," she said, revealing her one long black tooth, "you can take as many rampions as you like but . . . ." and here the witch paused significantly, ... "when your first child is born you must give it to me."

The man was so surprised and terrified that he muttered "Yes, yes, certainly" and ran back to his wife as fast as his legs could carry him.

Shortly after this a beautiful daughter was born to the wife and the witch promptly came and took her away to her house next door, despite the parents' heartrending tears and prayers.

The witch called the baby Flowerbell and she grew up to be a beautiful child with magnificent long golden tresses of hair.

When Flowerbell was twelve years old the witch carried her away to a far-off tower, hidden in the heart of a dense wood. The tower had no doors at all and the only way in was through a tiny window high up in the wall. Whenever the witch came to see Flowerbell she would cry out in a funny little voice:

> "*Flowerbell, Flowerbell,*
> *Let down your hair*
> *That I may climb*
> *As if by a stair.*"

And then the girl would take her long golden tresses, wind them round a stout hook fastened in the brickwork and let them drop to the ground. The witch would then use them as a ladder

83

to climb up to the little window. And so, in this lonely way, Flowerbell lived for several years.

One fine day a handsome young prince was riding through the wood on his nutbrown horse when he suddenly heard the sound of a voice singing quietly in the distance. The Prince followed the sound and finally arrived at the tower. For, as you may have guessed, it was the voice of Flowerbell singing to herself that he had heard. He rode his horse all round the tower but could find no way in. All he could see was the tiny window at the top. So he just stopped and listened to Flowerbell singing. And he came many a day afterwards to listen to her sweet voice. One day, however, when he was sitting on his horse, listening as usual, he saw the old witch come hobbling by. Hidden behind a tree he watched her as she called up:

> *"Flowerbell, Flowerbell,*
> *Let down your hair*
> *That I may climb*
> *As if by a stair."*

He saw the golden tresses come tumbling down and watched the witch climb nimbly up to the high window and disappear inside.

"Aha!" thought our handsome young Prince. "I shall try that tomorrow."

So the very next evening he went and stood under the tower and called out:

> *"Flowerbell, Flowerbell,*
> *Let down your hair*
> *That I may climb*
> *As if by a stair."*

Down came those splendid golden tresses, and up climbed the Prince on the silken ladder and slipped through the tiny window.

84

Flowerbell

Flowerbell was rather scared when she saw the handsome young Prince, for she had never set eyes on a man before.

"Don't be afraid," said the Prince gently. "I felt I had to come up to see who was singing so sweetly."

Flowerbell smiled happily and said: "I shall always sing for you, you seem so kind and gentle."

The next night the Prince returned once more to the tower and talked for a long time with Flowerbell. And after that Flowerbell looked forward to his coming each evening, for she felt very happy with him.

One day the Prince said to her: "Will you come away with me and be my wife?"

Flowerbell smiled sadly and said, "But how can I climb down from this lofty tower?" They sat in silence for a long while and suddenly Flowerbell's face lit up and she said, "I have an idea. If you bring me some silken cord each evening I will weave it into a ladder. Then I can climb down and you can carry me away with you on your horse."

So every evening the Prince came with a skein of silk. And every day Flowerbell worked hard to weave it into a long ladder. The ladder got longer and longer and Flowerbell became more excited at the thought that it would soon be finished and she would be riding away happily with her prince.

One day, however, she got so excited that she forgot herself and said to the witch:

"How is it that you take so long to climb the ladder when the Prince comes up in a flash . . . . . oh dear . . ."

"What's that you say, wicked child? What do I hear? Do my ears deceive me?" shrieked the witch in a tremendous fury and rage. "Have you been playing a trick on me behind my back? Who's this Prince, eh?"

And saying this she grabbed Flowerbell's hair, seized a pair of great scissors and swish, swosh, swish, the magnificent golden

Flowerbell

tresses lay on the floor. And what a sorry sight they presented!
And Flowerbell wept so much, she thought her little heart
would burst. The witch paid no attention whatsoever and
bundled the poor girl off to a dark lonely place in the woods,
far away from all other human beings. The cunning witch
was still not satisfied, however. She wanted to punish the Prince
as well. So that same evening she fastened Flowerbell's long
plaits to the window hook on the tower wall and when the Prince
called up to the window as usual she let them drop to the ground.

You can imagine the Prince's shock when he got to the top.
Not sweet little Flowerbell but the furious witch was there to
meet him, her eyes almost spitting fire.

"Aha!" she taunted, "I'm afraid your dear sweetheart is not
in. The wild cats have carried her away. I don't think you will
ever see her again for those same cats are going to scratch your
eyes out."

The Prince felt quite desperate and leapt out of the window
but he fell into such a dense bed of spiky thorns that he could
hardly get out and when he finally did he found that he was
blind.

So the poor young man wandered about for weeks and weeks
and months and months, eating only herbs and berries, and
weeping for the loss of dear Flowerbell.

Early one fine morning, as he wandered sadly along, he
heard the distant sound of sweet singing. Immediately he
recognized the voice of Flowerbell and he directed his steps
accordingly. Flowerbell saw him from a long way off and hurried
towards him weeping with joy. Two of her tears fell on the
Prince's eyes as he took her in his arms and, wonderful to relate,
he found he could see once more just as well as before!

How happy they were now! So he found his horse and off
they rode together to his kingdom and lived happily ever after.

The Broom

———————————*———————————

There was once a poor crossing-sweeper whose name was
Peter.

He lived rather a long time ago when even in quite
big towns the roads were ill-made, so that in bad weather they
got terribly muddy and dirty.

In the summer-time he did not have much to do, but there
was always dust and paper about, and even in summer it rains
sometimes—doesn't it?

He didn't earn a great deal of money.

Some people were too busy to heed him, and some were too
selfish, and some too poor to give him anything.

He had, however, a cheerful heart, and managed somehow
to make enough to pay the rent and to provide food and clothing
for himself and his wife and his little son.

One cold winter's day he had taken rather more pennies than
usual and went to get a cup of coffee from a coffee stall not very
far from his crossing, before starting on his way home.

He put his broom in a dark corner inside some railings where
he often left it if he went away for a few minutes. Now, oddly
enough, it happened that someone else had left a broom inside
those railings. It was just the same size and shape as his own, and
as it was nearly dark he never saw that there were two, and he
got hold of the wrong one and went off home with it.

The Broom

He put it down in the corner of the yard and went into the house to have his tea with his wife and little son.

Early the next morning, as he was getting dressed, he chanced to put his head out of the window.

There was his little son, who was only six years old, playing in the yard with the broom. He had his legs astride it, and was pretending it was a horse.

"Gee-up, gee-up," he said. And really the broom seemed to be prancing and leaping in the strangest way. "Almost as if it were really alive," thought Peter.

And just as he was thinking that, his little son called out: "Now then, up you go. Over the wall, Beauty!"

And—would you believe it?—the astonished Peter actually saw the broom rise up, with the boy still astride it, and fly over the wall into the next-door yard.

He rushed downstairs, half dressed as he was, ran through the gate, and into his neighbour's yard.

There he found his little boy, safe and sound on the ground, still astride the broom, laughing with joy and excitement.

"Good Beauty, good Beauty," he said.

But Peter stood staring in utter astonishment.

The Broom

"Mother, mother," he called, when he could speak. "Come quick, the broom's bewitched."

You can imagine what a to-do there was, and how all the neighbours came flocking round to see.

Every one had some different suggestion to make as to how the broom came to be bewitched.

They stood round in a circle looking at it lying in Peter's neighbour's yard, for no one dared to pick it up at first.

But presently Peter plucked up his courage and took hold of it, and seeing that nothing happened to him, his wife took it up in her turn. She turned it round in her hands.

"Why, Peter," she said, "this is not your broom at all. Don't you remember the brown burnt mark it got when it fell across the kitchen grate? That mark's not on this broom handle. You've got some one else's broom by mistake."

"It's my belief," said the little dried-up brown cobbler from the end cottage, "it's my belief it's a witch's broom. I'd have nothing to do with it if I were you, Peter. I should advise you to put it back where you got it from. Maybe your own broom is still there."

So Peter went off to look for his own broom, but he found it had disappeared.

He brought the other one home again.

"What shall we do?" he said to his wife when he came back. "I can't afford to buy a new broom; but I'm a bit afraid of this one. I dare say it really is a witch's broom. Don't you think it would be best to throw it away?"

But Peter's wife was a careful woman.

"No," she said. "Now we've got it, I reckon we'd better stick to it. It may bring good fortune. Who knows?"

So they kept the broom, and soon it brought them good fortune indeed for they quickly found out that it went wherever it was told to go by the person sitting astride it.

The Broom

It was really a most marvellous thing.

Peter and his son went riding on it all day long at first, then other people had a ride; soon the whole neighbourhood knew of Peter's wonderful broom.

Presently it began to bring in money. People who wanted to get anywhere in a hurry would come in and arrange to go on the broom. They paid handsomely. It was so convenient, as you can imagine. And much quicker than any other way, for motor cars and aeroplanes were not yet invented.

Peter began to grow rich. He moved into a bigger house with a little garden in front; he bought new clothes for his wife and the boy; he even talked of going up to London, where he felt sure he would earn more money with the wonderful broom. He no longer swept a crossing, and they had meat for dinner every day, and a whole roast chicken for dinner on Sundays.

The whole town knew about him and his good luck.

Strangers coming into the place would stare in astonishment at the sight of somebody sailing through the air on a broomstick.

"That's Peter's broom," the townsfolk would explain. "You can hire it out for a shilling an hour if you're lucky enough to find it idle."

One day a great scientist came to stay in Peter's town. He was a very great scientist indeed, and he spent his time finding out things about the moon. He was very much interested in the moon. And when he heard about the broom he went nearly mad with excitement.

"Now I shall be able to go and see what the moon is really like," he said.

Peter wasn't sure whether he liked the idea of the broom making such a long journey; but his wife persuaded him to consent.

"It will take him many hours to get to the moon," she said.

The Broom

"Think what a lot of shillings that will mean. And what harm can he come to?"

So Peter consented, and the scientist set off.

It took him a good long time to reach the moon, and when he got there the very first person he saw was the witch to whom the broom belonged, for, of course, it was a witch's broom, as you will already have guessed.

She was sitting on the very edge of the moon in a very bad temper. You see, it's very annoying for a witch to lose her broom; it is her chief way of getting about, and without it she has to depend either upon friendly lifts or upon whatever witchcraft she can think of to help her.

And a broom is so much simpler.

The minute the scientist alighted she saw that he had come up on her broom.

"You wicked old thief," she said, "how dare you steal my broom? How dare you go riding about on it in that brazen way? And me, the rightful owner, crawling all the way up on a miserable moonbeam. How dare you! I'll put a curse on you, I will. I'll put an end to you, I will. I'll broom you, you wicked old greybeard!"

The scientist was very frightened indeed, for witches are alarming at the best of times, and when they're angry . . . . .

He backed and backed, and before he knew what was happening he had fallen off the edge of the moon, down, down, down— and then, plop into the middle of the sea.

As good luck would have it, he was seen falling by the look-out man on a vessel, and was hauled in and given dry clothes and a hot drink and was not much the worse.

But he was bitterly disappointed.

Of course it was very hard.

Think of having a chance of seeing the moon at close quarters after studying it for years and years from far off, and then being

The Broom

chased off it by an old witch. And it wasn't his fault, either.

He was a nice old scientist. He went back to find Peter and to pay him for the hire of the broom, and to explain what had happened. Of course Peter couldn't blame him. After all, the broom wasn't really his either.

However, thanks to his careful wife, he had already saved enough money to be able to live quite comfortably ever after, so he didn't do so badly after all—did he now?

The Little Jackal and the Alligator

———————————✱———————————

The little Jackal was very fond of shell-fish. He used to go down by the river and hunt along the edges for crabs and such things. And once, when he was hunting for crabs, he was so hungry that he put his paw into the water after a crab without looking first—which you never should do! The minute he put in his paw, snap!—the big Alligator who lives in the mud down there had it in his jaws.

"Oh, dear!" thought the little Jackal; "the big Alligator has my paw in his mouth! In another minute he will pull me down and gobble me up! What shall I do? What shall I do?" Then he thought, suddenly, "I'll deceive him!"

So he put on a very cheerful voice, as if nothing at all were the matter, and he said:

"Ho! Ho! Clever Mr. Alligator! Smart Mr. Alligator, to take that old bulrush root for my paw! I hope you'll find it very tender!"

The old Alligator was hidden away beneath the mud and bulrush leaves, and he couldn't see anything. He thought, "Pshw! I've made a mistake." So he opened his mouth and let the little Jackal go.

The little Jackal ran away as fast as he could, and as he ran he called out—"Thank you, Mr. Alligator! Kind Mr. Alligator! So kind of you to let me go!"

The Little Jackal and the Alligator

The old Alligator lashed with his tail and snapped with his jaws, but it was too late; the little Jackal was out of reach.

After this the little Jackal kept away from the river, out of danger. But after about a week he got such an appetite for crabs that nothing else would do at all; he felt that he must have a crab. So he went down by the river and looked all around, very carefully. He didn't see the old Alligator, but he thought to himself, "I think I'll not take any chances." So he stood still and began to talk out loud to himself. He said:

"When I don't see any little crabs on the land I generally see them sticking out of the water, and then I put my paw in and catch them. I wonder if there are any fat little crabs in the water to-day?"

The old Alligator was hidden down in the mud at the bottom of the river, and when he heard what the little Jackal said, he thought, "Aha! I'll pretend to be a little crab, and when he puts his paw in, I'll make my dinner of him." So he stuck the black end of his snout above the water and waited.

The little Jackal took one look and then he said:

"Thank you, Mr. Alligator! Kind Mr. Alligator! You are exceedingly kind to show me where you are. I will have dinner elsewhere." And he ran away like the wind.

The old Alligator foamed at the mouth, he was so angry, but the little Jackal was gone.

For two whole weeks the little Jackal kept away from the river. Then, one day he got a feeling inside him that nothing but crabs could satisfy; he felt that he must have at least one crab. Very cautiously, he went down to the river and looked all around. He saw no sign of the old Alligator. Still, he did not mean to take any chances. So he stood quite still and began to talk to himself,—it was a little way he had. He said:

"When I don't see any little crabs on the shore, or sticking up out of the water, I usually see them blowing bubbles from under the water; and the little bubbles go puff, puff, puff, and then they go pop, pop, pop, and they show me where the little juicy crabs are, so I can put my paw in and catch them. I wonder if I shall see any little bubbles to-day?"

The old Alligator, lying low in the mud and weeds, heard this, and he thought, "Pooh! That's easy enough; I'll just blow some little crab-bubbles, and then he will put his paw in where I can get it."

So he blew, and he blew, a mighty blast, and the bubbles rose in a perfect whirlpool, fizzing and swirling.

The little Jackal didn't have to be told who was underneath those bubbles: he took one quick look, and off he ran. But as he went, he sang:

"Thank you, Mr. Alligator! Kind Mr. Alligator! You are the kindest Alligator in the world, to show me where you are, so nicely! I'll breakfast at another part of the river."

The old Alligator was so furious that he crawled up on the bank and went after the little Jackal; but, dear, dear, he couldn't catch the little Jackal; he ran far too fast.

After this, the little Jackal did not like to risk going near the water, so he ate no more crabs. But he found a garden of wild figs, which were so good that he went there every day, and ate them instead of shell-fish.

Now the old Alligator found this out, and he made up his mind to have the little Jackal for supper, or to die trying. So he crept, and crawled, and dragged himself over the ground to the garden of wild figs. There he made a huge pile of figs under the biggest of the wild fig trees, and hid himself in the pile.

After a while the little Jackal came dancing into the garden, very happy and free from care—but looking all around. He saw the huge pile of figs under the big fig tree.

"H'm," he thought, "that looks singularly like my friend, the Alligator. I'll investigate a bit."

The Little Jackal and the Alligator

He stood quite still and began to talk to himself—it was a little way he had. He said:

"The little figs I like best are the fat, ripe, juicy ones that drop off when the breeze blows; and then the wind blows them about on the ground, this way and that; the great heap of figs over there is so still that I think they must be all bad figs."

The old Alligator, underneath his fig pile, thought:

"Bother the suspicious little Jackal! I shall have to make these figs roll about, so that he will think the wind moves them." And straightway he humped himself up and moved, and sent the little figs flying—and his back showed through.

The little Jackal did not wait for a second look. He ran out of the garden like the wind. But as he ran he called back:

"Thank you, again, Mr. Alligator; very sweet of you to show me where you are; I can't stay to thank you as I should like: good-bye!"

At this the old Alligator was beside himself with rage. He vowed that he would have the little Jackal for supper this time, come what might. So he crept and crawled over the ground till he came to the little Jackal's house. Then he crept and crawled inside, and hid himself there in the house, to wait till the little Jackal should come home.

By and by the little Jackal came dancing home, happy and free from care—but looking all around. Presently, as he came along, he saw that the ground was all raked up as if something very heavy had been dragged over it. The little Jackal stopped and looked.

"What's this? What's this?" he said.

Then he saw that the door of his house was crushed at the sides and broken, as if something very big had gone through it.

"What's this? What's this?" the little Jackal said. "I think I'll investigate a little!"

The Little Jackal and the Alligator

So he stood quite still and began to talk to himself (you remember it was a little way he had), but loudly. He said:

"How strange that my little House doesn't speak to me! Why don't you speak to me, little House? You always speak to me, if everything is all right, when I come home. I wonder if anything is wrong with my little House?"

The old Alligator thought to himself that he must certainly pretend to be the little House, or the little Jackal would never come in. So he put on as pleasant a voice as he could (which is not saying much) and said:

"Hullo, little Jackal!"

Oh! When the little Jackal heard that, he was frightened enough, for once.

"It's the old Alligator," he said, "and if I don't make an end of him this time he will certainly make an end of me. What shall I do?"

He thought very fast. Then he spoke out pleasantly.

"Thank you, little House," he said, "it's good to hear your pretty voice, dear little House, and I will be in with you in a minute; only first I must gather some firewood for dinner."

Then he went and gathered firewood, and more firewood, and more firewood; and he piled it all up solid against the door and round the house; and then he set fire to it!

And it smoked and burned till it smoked that old Alligator to smoked herring!

Cap o' Rushes

———————————*———————————

One day long long ago there lived a very rich man who had three daughters. He thought to himself, "I wonder which of them loves me most?" So he called them to him and he said to the first:

"How much do you love me, my dear?"

"As much as I love my own life, father," replied she.

"Good," said the man. Then he turned to his second daughter.

"How much do *you* love me, my dear?"

"Better than anything in the world, father," replied she.

"Good," said the man and turning to his youngest daughter he asked:

"How much do *you* love me, my dear?"

"I love you as fresh meat needs salt," she replied.

"What! What!" cried the father angrily. "What do you mean? You don't love me at all, do you? Leave this house and never return again!" And he drove her away.

The youngest daughter was very sad indeed, for she knew she loved her father dearly. She wandered over the countryside and through the fields till she came to a stream. Here she plucked an armful of green rushes and wove them together into a kind of cloak and hood and she put them on so that you couldn't see what a fine gown she was wearing underneath. And then she walked on till she arrived at a large house not far away. She knocked at the door and asked whether they could give her any work. They were kind enough to take her in as a kitchen-maid. And so Cap o' Rushes (as everyone called her now) spent all her time scouring pots and pans for the cook.

Cap o' Rushes

Not very long afterwards the master of this house gave a huge party to which he invited all his friends. There was a lot of extra work for Cap o' Rushes to do and there was no counting the number of pots and pans she had to scour.

In the evening all the servants went to watch the feasting and dancing, except Cap o' Rushes, who said she preferred to stay behind. But when all the other servants had gone, Cap o' Rushes took off her cloak and hood, put on a beautiful golden dress and went in—not to watch—but to join all the other splendid visitors. Everybody thought how lovely she looked and wondered who on earth she could be. The handsome young son of the master of the house could not take his eyes off her and fell head over heels in love with her. He asked her to dance and from then on did not leave her side the whole evening.

However, Cap o' Rushes managed to slip away and left the feast before it ended. When she got back to the servants' rooms she put on her cloak and hood once more and was fast asleep by the time the others got back. The next morning they began telling Cap o' Rushes all about the magnificent party.

"Oh my!" said the cook, "you really should have seen all the fine ladies and gentlemen at the party last night. And especially the *beautiful* young lady in the golden dress! The master's son danced with her the whole evening!"

Cap o' Rushes smiled but said not a word and went on scouring her pots and pans.

In the meantime the master's son was trying to find out who his lovely dancing partner was and where she lived. But nobody could tell him. So he persuaded his father to give another ball, hoping that she could come again. "There's another dance this evening," the cook told Cap o' Rushes. Cap o' Rushes said she felt too tired to go. But when the evening came and all the servants had gone, she took off her cap o' rushes and put on a beautiful silver dress and off she went to the dance. The master's son was delighted to see her again and danced with her all the evening. But once more Cap o' Rushes managed to slip away just before the end.

And when the other servants arrived she was asleep with her cap o' rushes on.

Next morning the cook said to her: "What a shame you didn't come with us to watch the ball last night. That beautiful lady was there again, with a silver dress this time, and the young master didn't leave her side for one moment."

"Oh," said Cap o' Rushes with a smile, "I should indeed like to have seen her."

Meanwhile the master's son had been looking everywhere to find out where the beautiful young lady lived and as he could not find her anywhere he asked his father to give another ball.

Again all the servants tried to persuade Cap o' Rushes to come along with them, but she said she was too tired. But as soon as they had left she took off cap and cloak and put on a dress of pure, pure white and off she went to the ball.

You can imagine how delighted the master's son was to see her again. As he danced with her he kept asking her name and where she came from. And when she wouldn't tell him he gave her a ring and said he would die if he didn't ever see her again.

But once more, when the last dance was over, Cap o' Rushes slipped off to the servants' rooms and by the time the others were back she was asleep with her cap o' rushes on.

The next day the cook said to her:

"A great pity you didn't come to the dance. That young girl was wearing a dress of pure, pure white. She was so lovely that the young master didn't leave her for a moment. But you won't have another chance of seeing her for there are to be no more dances."

The master's son sent around everywhere asking where the lovely young lady might be and whether anybody knew her.

Cap o' Rushes

But there was no news of her at all. He grew quite ill because he was so sad, until finally he got a fever and had to be kept in bed.

One day the cook was making some special light porridge for the young master's breakfast when Cap o' Rushes walked into the kitchen.

"And who are you making that for, cook?" she asked.

"It's for the young master. He's very ill, dying for the love of his lady."

"Oh, please let *me* make it," said Cap o' Rushes. And while she was doing so she slipped into it the ring that the young master had given her at the last ball.

A maid took the porridge up to the young master's room and when he had drunk it he saw the ring on the bottom of the dish.

"Send for the cook," he said to the maid.

And when she came up he said:

"Who prepared this porridge?"

"I did, master," said the cook, very alarmed.

"No you didn't," said the young master. "Tell me who did and no harm will come to you."

"I made it, truly, master, truly I did, but Cap o' Rushes helped me and it was she who poured it into your porridge bowl."

"Ah!" said the young master, his face lighting up. "Send Cap o' Rushes up to me at once." So off went the cook and sent Cap o' Rushes up to the young master's room.

"Did you help to make this porridge and pour it into my porridge bowl?" he asked.

"Yes, I did," she said.

"And where did you get this ring?" asked the young master, holding it up.

"From the man who gave it to me," replied she.

"Well, who are you then?" asked the young master in surprise.

Cap o' Rushes

Then she slipped off her cap and cloak and stood there in her beautiful golden dress.

The master's son was now very happy and soon got quite well again. They started to prepare for their wedding and hundreds of guests were invited from far and wide. And an invitation was sent to Cap o' Rushes's father.

Before the wedding feast Cap o' Rushes went to the cook and said: "I don't want you to put even the tiniest grain of salt in the meat."

"That wouldn't be a very nice thing to do," said the cook. "The meat won't have any taste."

"Never mind," said Cap o' Rushes, "just do as I ask, just for this once. I have a special reason."

Very soon all the guests came into the banqueting hall, following the bride and bridegroom.

When the meat course was served hardly anyone touched it, it was too tasteless. But one particular guest, a rich gentleman, burst out crying.

"What is the matter, sir?" the master's son asked him.

"Ah," he replied sadly, "I had a daughter once and I asked her how much she loved me. And she said: 'As much as fresh meat needs salt.' And I drove her out of my house and I've never seen her since. But now I see she loved me best of all. And I may never see her again." And he wept loudly.

"No, father, here I am," cried Cap o' Rushes. Moving aside her bridal veil she ran up to him and flung her arms around his neck. Her father was overcome with joy and everyone was very happy indeed. And that is the end of my story.

Henny-Penny

————————————*————————————

One morning Henny-Penny was pecking corn in the garden when—BANG! an acorn fell down from the sky and hit her right on the head

"Goodness gracious me!" said Henny-Penny. "The sky's going to fall, I had better go and tell the King."

So off went Henny-Penny and after a while she met Cocky-Locky.

"Good-day, Cocky-Locky," she said.

"And a good-day to you, Henny-Penny," said Cocky-Locky. "And where may you be going so early in the morning?"

"I'm off to tell the King that the sky is falling," said Henny-Penny.

"May I come with you?" said Cocky-Locky.

"Of course you may," said Henny-Penny.

So Henny-Penny and Cocky-Locky went along together to tell the King the sky was falling. They went on and on and on until after a while they met Ducky-Daddles.

"And where may you two be going, Henny-Penny and Cocky-Locky?" asked Ducky-Daddles.

"We're off to tell the King the sky is falling," said Henny-Penny and Cocky-Locky.

"May I come with you?" said Ducky-Daddles.

"Of course you may," said Henny-Penny and Cocky-Locky.

So Henny-Penny and Cocky-Locky and Ducky-Daddles went along together to tell the King the sky was falling. They went on and on and on until after a while they met Goosey-Poosey.

"And where may you be going to, Henny-Penny, Cocky-Locky and Ducky-Daddles?" asked Goosey-Poosey.

"We're off to tell the King the sky is falling," said Henny-Penny, Cocky-Locky and Ducky-Daddles.

"May I come with you?" asked Goosey-Poosey.

"Of course you may," said Henny-Penny, Cocky-Locky and Ducky-Daddles.

So Henny-Penny, Cocky-Locky, Ducky-Daddles and Goosey-Poosey went off together to tell the King the sky was falling. They walked on and on and on until after a while they met Turkey-Lurkey.

"And where may you be going to, Henny-Penny, Cocky-Locky, Ducky-Daddles and Goosy-Poosey?" asked Turkey-Lurkey.

"We're going to tell the King the sky's falling," said Henny-Penny, Cockey-Locky, Ducky-Daddles and Goosey-Poosey.

"May I come with you?" asked Turkey-Lurkey.

"Of course you may," said Henny-Penny, Cocky-Locky, Ducky-Daddles and Goosey-Poosey.

So Henny-Penny, Cocky-Locky, Ducky-Daddles, Goosey-Poosey and Turkey-Lurkey all went off together to tell the King the sky was falling. And they walked on and on until after a while they met Foxy-Woxy.

"And where may all of you be going to this fine morning, Henny-Penny, Cocky-Locky, Ducky-Daddles, Goosey-Poosey and Turkey-Lurkey?" asked Foxy-Woxy.

"If you really must know," said Henny-Penny, Cocky-Locky, Ducky-Daddles, Goosey-Poosey and Turkey-Lurkey, "We're all off to tell the King that the sky is falling."

Henny-Penny

"But oh," said Foxy-Woxy, "but oh, this isn't the way to where the King lives, Henny-Penny, Cocky-Locky, Ducky-Daddles, Goosey-Poosey and Turkey-Lurkey. If you follow me, I'll show you the right way. Would you all like to come with me?"

"Oh, that is indeed very kind of you, Foxy-Woxy," said Henny-Penny, Cocky-Locky, Ducky-Daddles, Goosey-Poosey and Turkey-Lurkey.

So Henny-Penny, Cocky-Locky, Ducky-Daddles, Goosey-Poosey, Turkey-Lurkey and Foxy-Woxy all went along together to tell the King that the sky was falling. And they went on and on and on until after a while they came to a dark, dark hole.

Now this dark, dark hole was really the door of Foxy-Woxy's den. But of course, Foxy-Woxy was too foxy to let them know this. Instead he said: "This is a short cut to where the King lives. If you follow me we'll get there in next to no time. Let me go first and you come after me, Henny-Penny, Cocky-Locky, Ducky-Daddles, Goosey-Poosey and Turkey-Lurkey."

"Why, of course we'll follow you, of course, of course," replied Henny-Penny, Cocky-Locky, Ducky-Daddles, Goosey-Poosey and Turkey-Lurkey.

So Foxy-Woxy went into his dark, dark den but he didn't go very far inside the dark, dark den. Instead he turned round and waited for Henny-Penny, Cocky-Locky, Ducky-Daddles, Goosey-Poosey and Turkey-Lurkey to follow in after him.

What Foxy-Woxy meant to do when they were all inside was to eat them all up. But luckily for Henny-Penny, Cocky-Locky, Ducky-Daddles, Goosey-Poosey and Turkey-Lurkey, just as they were about to go into the dark cave, a little bird, perched on a branch of a tree, saw them all and guessed what was going to happen. So he called out very loudly:

"Be careful, Henny-Penny, Cocky-Locky, Ducky-Daddles, Goosey-Poosey and Turkey-Lurkey. If you don't want Foxy-

Henny-Penny

Woxy to eat you all up, you'd better turn back and run home as fast as you can."

And only just in time they all turned back and ran home as fast as ever they could. So old Foxy-Woxy didn't have his nice dinner after all. And the King never knew that they thought the sky was going to fall.

The Sleeping Beauty

―――――――――――――*―――――――――――――

Long long ago a beautiful baby daughter was born to a King and Queen. They were so full of joy that they decided to celebrate the christening with a great feast and to invite the seven chief fairies in the land to act as godmothers.

One by one the fairies stepped up to the baby's cradle and, waving a magic wand, presented the princess with a gift. And the first one said that she should be the most beautiful princess that ever lived; the second, that she should be the wisest; the third, that she should be most graceful; the fourth that she should sing as sweetly as the nightingale; the fifth that she should dance like a fairy, and the sixth that she should be able to play every known musical instrument.

And now it was the turn of the seventh and last fairy, but just as she was about to step forward a very wicked, crooked, humpbacked fairy stepped in front of her with an evil smile on her face. The King had not invited this fairy to the christening, so she came to cast an evil spell on the baby and this is what she said:

"When the princess is fifteen years old she shall prick her finger with a spindle and die."

A terrible silence fell on the guests and the Queen began to weep.

As the wicked fairy hobbled away, the seventh and last good fairy stood beside the cradle and said:

The Sleeping Beauty

"The baby will not die. The princess will indeed prick her finger in a spindle but I promise you that she will only fall into a deep sleep which will last a hundred years. Then a prince will come and waken her with a kiss."

Then all the guests went home, but the King immediately sent out orders that nobody in the land should be allowed to have a spindle and that all spindles should be destroyed. By doing this the King thought that the terrible thing foretold by the wicked fairy would never happen, for there would positively be no spindles for the princess to prick her pretty finger on.

The royal baby grew up to be a beautiful girl, knowing nothing about the terrible spell that had been cast upon her.

Fifteen years went by happily and one day the princess was playing hide and seek with her friends in the wood. She happened to wander and came to a tower that she had never seen before. She found herself climbing a narrow, winding staircase till she came to a tiny little room right at the top. Inside was a tiny old woman twisting her thread round a—SPINDLE. This woman was so old and deaf that she had never heard of the King's command to destroy all spindles.

Suddenly the princess felt that at all costs she must hold the spindle in her hand and she begged the old woman to give it to her. The old woman understood and let the princess hold it. And of course the princess immediately pricked her finger and fell to the ground fast asleep.

The old woman, very frightened, climbed slowly down the narrow, winding staircase to look for help. People came running from all parts to see what they could do; they threw water in her face, they unlaced her dress and slapped her hands—but all in vain. Then the King's Chief Adviser remembered what the good fairy had foretold. So the King ordered the princess to be carried to the most splendid room in the palace and to be laid on a bed embroidered with silver and gold and silk and satin. No one was to disturb her.

When the good fairy heard what had happened she was, of course, not in the least surprised. She simply waved her magic wand and everybody—everybody, including the princess's pet dog and cat and the horses in the stables—all fell into a deep sleep.

Then she waved her wand once more and immediately the palace and all its parts were surrounded by dense trees and bushes and brambles and thorns. Nothing could be seen of the castle except its golden turrets peeping out above the tall trees.

And now many, many, long years passed—twenty, fifty, a hundred—and a handsome young prince came riding to those parts, hunting wild deer. Suddenly he found himself in the midst of a dense wood. He thought he was quite lost when he caught sight of the golden turrets of the castle gleaming above the tree-tops.

"How strange!" he thought. "I wonder who lives there shut away from the rest of the world."

He asked an old woodcutter about it.

"Ah!" replied the old man, "there is indeed something mysterious about that castle. 'Tis said that a beautiful princess lies sleeping there; ay! she's been sleeping there for many a long year under the spell of some fairy. No doubt, a handsome young man like yourself could break the spell by rescuing her."

"Yes," murmured the prince as he galloped off. "Maybe I can break the spell." And he forced his way through thorns and bushes and brambles and briars. After a very, very long time he at last arrived at the castle. But everything was deathly still. Dogs and horses and farm animals and even spiders all seemed to be fast asleep.

Inside he was amazed to find the servants still as statues over

The Sleeping Beauty

their work. The prince could feel that a powerful spell was at work.

He walked through room after room, climbed marble stairway after marble stairway. Suddenly through a blaze of sunlight he saw the most beautiful girl he had ever seen, clad in rich robes, lying asleep on a bed of satin and gold.

The prince tiptoed quietly in, bent over and gently kissed her ruby lips. At once the princess opened her beautiful blue eyes and sat up. "Oh!" she exclaimed. "What a wonderful dream I have had!" And at the same time the prince could hear the sound of bustle and movement throughout the castle and its grounds—the barking of dogs, the whinnying of horses, the mooing of cows, and all the noises of farm animals and the palace pets.

The Sleeping Beauty

The prince took the arm of the young princess and they walked down the marble staircase together. At the foot of the stairs stood the King and Queen waiting for them with radiant smiles and shining eyes, for they too had awoken with the coming of the prince. And so, soon after, the prince and princess were married and they all lived happily ever after.

The Adventures of the Little Field Mouse

————————————*————————————

Once upon a time, there was a little brown Field Mouse; and one day he was out in the fields to see what he could find. He was running along in the grass, poking his nose into everything and looking with his two eyes all about, when he saw a smooth, shiny acorn lying in the grass. It was such a fine shiny little acorn that he thought he would take it home with him; so he put out his paw to touch it, but the little acorn rolled away from him. He ran after it, but it kept rolling on, just ahead of him, till it came to a place where a big oak-tree and its roots spread all over the ground. Then it rolled under a big, round root.

Little Mr. Field Mouse ran to the root and poked his nose under after the acorn, and there he saw a small round hole in the ground. He slipped through and saw some stairs going down into the earth. The acorn was rolling down, with a soft tapping sound, ahead of him, so down he went too. Down, down, down, rolled the acorn, and down, down, down, went the Field Mouse, until suddenly he saw a tiny door at the foot of the stairs.

The shiny acorn rolled to the door and struck against it with a tap. Quickly the little door opened and the acorn rolled inside. The Field Mouse hurried as fast as he could down the last stairs, and pushed through just as the door was closing. It shut behind him, and he was in a little room. And there, before him, stood a queer little Red Man! He had a little red cap, and a little red jacket, and odd little red shoes with points at the toes.

"You are my prisoner," he said to the Field Mouse.

"What for?" said the Field Mouse.

"Because you tried to steal my acorn," said the little Red Man.

"It is my acorn," said the Field Mouse; "I found it."

"No, it isn't," said the little Red Man, "I have it; you will never see it again."

The little Field Mouse looked all about the room as fast as he could, but he could not see any acorn. Then he thought he would go back up the tiny stairs to his own home. But the little door was locked and the little Red Man had the key. And he said to the poor Mouse, "You shall be my servant; you shall make my bed and sweep my room and cook my broth."

So the little brown Mouse was the little Red Man's servant, and every day he made the little Red Man's bed and swept the little Red Man's room and cooked the little Red Man's broth. And every day the little Red Man went away through the tiny door and did not come back till afternoon. But he always locked the door after him, and carried away the key.

At last, one day he was in such a hurry that he turned the key before the door was quite latched, which, of course, didn't lock it at all. He went away without noticing—he was in such a hurry.

The little Field Mouse knew that his chance had come to run away home. But he didn't want to go without the pretty, shiny acorn. Where it was he didn't know, so he looked everywhere. He opened every little drawer and looked in, but it wasn't in any of the drawers; he peeped on every shelf, but it wasn't on a shelf; he hunted in every closet, but it wasn't in there. Finally, he climbed up on a chair and opened a wee, wee door in the chimney piece—and there it was!

He took it quickly in his forepaws, and then he took it in his mouth, and then he ran away. He pushed open the little door; he climbed out up up the little stairs; he came out through the hole under the root; he ran and ran through the fields; and at last he came to his own house.

When he was in his own house he set the shiny acorn on the table. I expect he set it down hard, for all at once, with a little snap, it opened!—exactly like a little box.

And what do you think! There was a tiny necklace inside! It was a most beautiful tiny necklace, all made of jewels, and it was just big enough for a lady mouse. So the little Field Mouse gave the tiny necklace to his little Mouse-sister. She thought it was perfectly lovely. And when she wasn't wearing it she kept it in the shiny acorn box.

And the little Red Man never knew what had become of it, because he didn't know where the little Field Mouse lived.

The Discontented Pig

─────────────────────────────*─────────────────────────────

Ever so long ago, in the time when there were fairies, and men and animals talked together, there was a curly-tailed pig. He lived by himself in a house at the edge of the village, and every day he worked in his garden. Whether the sun shone or the rain fell he hoed and dug and weeded, turning the earth around his tomato vines and loosening the soil of the carrot plot, until word of his fine vegetables travelled through seven counties, and each year he won the royal prize at the fair.

But after a time that little pig grew tired of the endless toil.

"What matters it if I do have the finest vegetables in the kingdom," he thought, "since I must work myself to death getting them to grow? I mean to go out and see the world and find an easier way of making a living."

So he locked the door of his house and shut the gate of his garden and started down the road.

A good three miles he travelled, till he came to a cottage almost hidden in a grove of trees. Lovely music sounded around him and Little Pig smiled, for he had an ear for sweet sounds.

"I will go look for it," he said, following in the direction from which it seemed to come.

Now it happened that in that house dwelt Thomas, a cat, who made his living by playing on the violin. Little Pig saw him standing in the door pushing the bow up and down across the

The Discontented Pig

strings. It put a thought into his head. Surely this must be easier and far more pleasant than digging in a garden!

"Will you teach me to play the violin, friend cat?" asked Little Pig.

Thomas looked up from his bow and nodded his head.

"To be sure," he answered; "just do as I am doing."

And he gave him the bow and fiddle.

Little Pig took them and began to saw, but squeak! quang! No sweet music fell upon his ear. The sounds he heard were like the squealing of his baby brother pigs when a wolf came near them.

"Oh!" he cried, "this isn't music!"

Thomas the cat, nodded his head.

"Of course not," he said. "You haven't tried long enough. He who would play the violin must work."

"Then I think I'll look for something else," Piggywig answered, "because this is quite as hard as weeding my garden."

And he gave back the bow and fiddle and started down the road.

The Discontented Pig

He walked on and on, until he came to a hut where lived a dog who made cheese. He was kneading and moulding the curd into cakes, and Little Pig thought it looked quite easy.

"I think I'd like to go into the cheese business myself," he said to himself. So he asked the dog if he would teach him.

This the dog was quite willing to do, and a moment later Little Pig was working beside him.

Soon he grew hot and tired and stopped to rest and fan himself.

"No, no!" exclaimed the dog, "you will spoil the cheese. There can be no rest time until the work is done."

Little Pig opened his eyes in amazement.

"Indeed!" he replied. "Then this is just as hard as growing vegetables or learning to play a violin. I mean to look for something easier."

And he started down the road.

On the other side of the river, in a sweet green field, a man was taking honey out of beehives. Little Pig saw him as he crossed the bridge and thought that of all the trades he had seen this was what suited him best. It must be lovely there in the meadow among the flowers. Honey was not heavy to lift, and once in a while he could have a mouthful of it. He ran as fast as he could go to ask the man if he would take him into his employ.

This plan pleased the bee man as much as it pleased the pig.

"I've been looking for a helper for a year and a day," he said. "Begin work at once."

He gave Little Pig a veil and a pair of gloves, telling him to fasten them on well. Then he told him to lift a honey-comb out of a hive.

Little Pig ran to do it, twisting his curly tail in the joy of having at last found a business that suited him. But buzz, buzz! The bees crept under his veil and inside his gloves. They stung him on his fingers, his mouth, his ears, and the end of his nose, and he squealed and dropped the honey and ran.

"Come back, come back!" the man called.

"No, no!" Little Pig answered with a big squeal. "No, no, the bees hurt me!"

The man nodded his head.

"Of course they do," he said. "They hurt me too! That is part of the work. You cannot be a beekeeper without getting stung."

Little Pig blinked his beady eyes and began to think hard.

"It seems that every kind of work has something unpleasant about it. To play the violin you must practise until your arm aches. When you make cheese you dare not stop a minute until the work is done, and in taking honey from a hive, the bees sting you until your head is on fire. Work in my garden is not so bad after all, and I am going back to it."

So he said good-bye to the bee man and was soon back in his carrot patch. He hoed and raked and weeded, singing as he worked, and there was no more contented pig in all that kingdom. Every autumn he took his vegetables to the fair and brought home the royal prize, and sometimes, on holidays, the cat and the dog and the bee man came to call.

Silly Simon

———————————————*———————————————

Once upon a time there was a very rich man who had a beautiful daughter. But the beautiful daughter could neither speak nor laugh.

The best doctors in all the land came to see the girl and they said, "This girl cannot speak because she cannot laugh. If someone can make her laugh then she will be able to speak."

The rich man said, "If any man can make my daughter laugh, I shall give him a bag of silver and a bag of gold."

After that, a hundred men had tried to make the rich man's daughter laugh, but not one of them had been able to do so.

Now in this land, there was a common and on the edge of the common was a little house and in the little house lived a poor woman and her son.

All day long the poor woman sat spinning but her son did nothing at all.

In the summer he sat in the sunshine doing nothing at all and in the winter he sat by the fire doing nothing at all.

Everyone called him Silly Simon.

At last the poor woman could stand it no longer. She said, "It is time you did some work. Away with you across the common and see if you can find something to do."

The next morning, Silly Simon set off across the common and very soon he met a farmer.

Silly Simon

The farmer said, "I need a boy like you to drive the pigs. If you will drive the pigs I shall give you a penny."

So Silly Simon drove the farmer's pigs and at the end of the day the farmer gave him a bright, new penny.

Silly Simon held the penny in his hand and ran along home.

Silly Simon came to a stream and in the stream he saw silver fish and gold fish, but when he tried to catch a fish, his bright new penny slipped out of his hand and rolled into the stream.

When he got home, he told his mother what had happened.

"You stupid boy!" said his mother. "That is not the way to carry a penny. The way to carry a penny is to put it in your pocket and run along home. Now remember that!"

"Yes, I shall remember that," said Silly Simon.

On the second day, Silly Simon set off across the common and very soon he met a man with six cows.

The man said, "I need a boy like you to milk my cows. If you will milk my cows, I shall give you a jug of new milk." So Silly Simon milked the cows and at the end of the day the farmer gave him a jug of new milk.

Silly Simon said to himself, "Now what did my mother tell me? She said I was to put it in my pocket and run along home."

So he put the jug of milk in his pocket and he ran along home.

But when he got home his mother took the jug out of his pocket and there was not a drop of milk inside it. "You stupid boy!" said his mother. "That is not the way to carry a jug of milk. The way to carry a jug of milk is to hold it on your head and walk slowly home. Now remember that!"

"Yes, I shall remember that," said Silly Simon.

On the third day, Silly Simon set off across the common and very soon he met the farmer's wife.

The farmer's wife said, "I need a boy like you to feed my hens.

Silly Simon

If you will feed my hens, I shall give you a fresh cream cheese."
So Silly Simon fed the hens and at the end of the day the farmer's
wife gave him a fresh cream cheese. Silly Simon said to himself,
"Now what did my mother tell me? She said I was to carry it
on my head and walk slowly home."

So he put the fresh cream cheese on his head and walked home
slowly in the sunshine.

But the cream cheese melted away in the hot sunshine and
when his mother saw him, she said, "You stupid boy! That is not
the way to carry a fresh cream cheese. The way to carry a fresh
cream cheese is to hold it carefully in your hands and run along
home. Now remember that!"

"Yes, I shall remember that," said Silly Simon.

On the fourth day, Silly Simon set off across the common and
very soon he met a woodcutter.

The woodcutter said, "I need a boy like you to tie up my
sticks. If you will tie up my sticks, I shall give you a log of
wood."

So Silly Simon tied up the sticks and at the end of the day, the
woodcutter gave him a log of wood. Silly Simon said to himself,
"Now what did my mother tell me? She said I was to hold it
carefully in my hands and run along home."

So he held the log in his hands and tried to run home, but the
log was too heavy and he had to leave it at the side of the
road.

When his mother heard about this, she said, "You stupid boy!
That is not the way to carry a log of wood. The way to carry a
log of wood is to tie it with rope and pull it along home. Now
remember that!"

"Yes, I shall remember that," said Silly Simon.

On the fifth day, Silly Simon set off across the common and
very soon he met a butcher.

The butcher said, "I need a boy like you to sweep my floor. If

Silly Simon

you will sweep my floor, I shall give you a leg of mutton." So Silly Simon swept the floor and at the end of the day, the butcher gave him a leg of mutton. Silly Simon said to himself, "Now what did my mother tell me? She said I was to tie it with rope and pull it along home."

So he tied the leg of mutton with rope, put it on the ground and pulled it along home.

Now when his mother saw the leg of mutton all covered with dirt and dust, she said, "I do believe you are the stupidest boy in all the world. That is not the way to carry a leg of mutton. The way to carry a leg of mutton is to lift it on to your shoulder and come along home. Now remember that!"

"Yes, I shall remember that," said Silly Simon.

On the sixth day, Silly Simon set off across the common and very soon he met a man with four donkeys.

The man said, "I need a boy like you to clean the stables. If you will clean the stables, I shall give you a donkey."

So Silly Simon cleaned the stables and at the end of the day, the man gave him a donkey. Silly Simon said to himself, "Now what did my mother tell me? She said I was to lift it on to my shoulder and come along home."

So he lifted the great donkey on to his shoulder and set off for home.

Just then the rich man and his beautiful daughter passed by. When the beautiful daughter saw little Silly Simon carrying the great donkey on his shoulder, she began to laugh.

Then she said to her father, "Just look at that silly boy carrying a great donkey!"

The rich man said to Silly Simon, "You are the cleverest boy in the land because you have made my daughter laugh and speak. Here is a bag of silver and here is a bag of gold."

Silly Simon held the bag of gold in his right hand and the bag of silver in his left hand and ran along home as fast as he could run.

When his mother saw the silver and gold she said, "That is the way to carry bags of silver and gold. I always knew you were the cleverest boy in all the world."

The Mouse Bride

————————————————*————————————————

A farmer and his wife had no children . . . but one year, in the season of ploughing, a strange thing happened to them.

Each evening as he came to the end of his day's work, the Farmer would lean on his plough and lament aloud, "My neighbours all have sons who will plough their fields when they are old and feeble. But I have none. What will become of my land? Oh, if I only had a son! Oh, that a son would fall down from the sky!"

One evening—when he was saying this as usual—a hawk flew over his head, and wondering, I suppose, to hear an old man talking to himself, he spread his claws in surprise, and out there dropped a mouse . . . . a little mouse, a boy-mouse. And he fell at the feet of the Farmer.

The Farmer picked him up, saying, "Where have you come from?"

"Out of the sky," replied the Mouse simply.

"Will you come home with me?" asked the Farmer.

"Yes, sir, if you like," agreed the Mouse.

"Will you learn to plough and sow and reap?" continued the Farmer.

"My goodness, I can do that already!" squeaked the Mouse, very much amused.

The Mouse Bride

So the Farmer carried him home and set him down on the table. But when the Farmer's wife came in from the yard, she gave a piercing shriek.

"Look, husband, look!" she cried, clutching her sari around her. "Look, there's a mouse on the table!"

"That is our son," explained the Farmer gravely.

"A mouse! Our son!" exclaimed the wife.

For a moment she thought her husband had been out in the sun too long, and was raving.

"This little fellow dropped out of the sky," said the Farmer.

But the Mouse was very frightened. "Why is she shrieking?" he asked piteously.

"I do not know," replied the Farmer. "She was not expecting you—yes, that is it, she's taken by surprise. Enough!" he said to his wife, and gave her a shake to steady her.

But now she was really looking at the Mouse, and suddenly she smiled.

"Why, husband, you are right," she said; "yes, yes, it is our son."

And she hugged the boy-mouse and gave him food, then put him to bed. And in the morning she made him a little red coat, and he strode off into the fields with his newly-found father.

It was quite true what he had said, that he could plough and sow and reap. Very well he did it—some days better than the Farmer himself. Nothing could tire him. All day long he worked, ploughing late into the evening, his paws clenched on the handles of the plough, his face set in a frown, and his whiskers gleaming red with the setting sun.

Then the Farmer would call to him, "Come on, my dear, come home. Look how late it is."

The Mouse looked up at the sky, then answered steadily, "I can still see to plough, Father."

The Mouse Bride

"But, look, all my neighbours' sons have gone home to supper," said the Farmer.

"Have they all gone?" The Mouse looked round as he spoke. "Are the fields quite empty?"

"There's Rama in the next field, just packing up," was the reply.

"I shall plough until he has gone." And the Mouse gripped the handles of the plough, to show that he meant what he said.

"Don't tire yourself, my son." The Farmer spoke kindly, for he had grown to love his adopted son very deeply.

"I am a strong mouse," said the little creature.

Not until the fields were empty would he stop work, and when he got home he would be merry and sing to please his parents.

The Farmer was so proud of him; he thought there was no better son on earth. But after a time the little animal was no longer merry, he sang no more; and though he ploughed as well and as long as ever, he was a different mouse when he came home at night.

Then the Farmer was grieved, but his wife—who knew other things than ploughing—took a measure, and when the mouse was asleep, measured the length of his tail.

"Why are you doing that?" asked the Farmer.

"Hush!" replied the wife; "hush, and I will tell you. Seven inches—exactly. What's three times seven, husband?"

The Farmer thought for a moment. "Three sevens? Hmph! ... three sevens are twenty-one."

The Farmer's wife gave a delighted nod.

"Yes, yes, I thought so!" she whispered.

"What did you think?" the Farmer whispered back.

"Our little boy-mouse has become a man," she replied softly.

"A man!" echoed the Farmer. "But why is he sad?"

His wife put the measure away.

The Mouse Bride

"He is sad, husband, because he needs a wife," she said, and she looked tenderly at the sleeping mouse, who gave a tiny sigh as he snuggled in more cosily.

"If it's a wife he wants, I'll go and find him one," said the Farmer stoutly.

"Yes, tomorrow," agreed the woman. "But mind you, husband, she must be the best wife in the world to be worthy of our wonderful son."

The Farmer moved off towards the fire. "She must be like him, neither better nor worse," he grunted.

And so the very next day, the little man-mouse in his red coat, and the Farmer, his adopted father, set out to look for a wife. And all day long they searched and found no one. As the sun set, they sat down on a stone; the Farmer was quite worn out, and even the Mouse was beginning to yawn.

Suddenly, the Moon stepped up into the sky, dazzling the Farmer with her beauty.

"Look, look, my son!" he cried. "There is a wife worthy of you. What do you think of her?"

The Mouse looked up at the Moon until he blinked. She was bright, she was radiant, but he did not much care for her.

So he turned to the Farmer, and said, "True, she is very beautiful, Father, but she is so cold and proud."

"Yes, I am cold," scoffed the Moon; "I am proud. I am not for you."

The Farmer got up and made a deep salaam. "Tell me, my Lady Moon, is there none better than you?"

"Oh yes," replied the Moon, "There is the cloud. When she covers me with her mantle I am invisible. She is better than I."

At that moment a cloud slipped over the Moon, and hid her from sight.

"Look, look, my son!" said the Farmer. "There is a wife worthy of you. What do you think of her?"

The Mouse Bride

"She is very fine," agreed the Mouse. "But she's sad and gloomy."

"Tell me, Lady Cloud," said the Farmer, "is there none better than you?"

"Oh, yes!" replied the Cloud, "there is the Wind. She drives me all round the sky. She is better than I."

And at once the Wind blew hard, and scattered the Cloud.

And now the Farmer thought he had found a fine wife for the Mouse, and said, "The Wind now! She's just the one for you. What do you think of her?"

The Mouse shivered. "She sets my whiskers a-flutter, father, but she fidgets so," he complained.

"Yes, I am restless," whistled the Wind. "I am not for you."

"Tell me, Lady Wind," said the Farmer, "is there none better than you?"

"The Mountain," replied the Wind promptly. "She is far better than I, for although I storm, I cannot move her."

And the Farmer and the Mouse turned round, and saw that they were sitting at the foot of a mighty mountain.

"There!" exclaimed the Farmer with relief. "At last we have found a wife worthy of you. Now then what do you think of her?"

"She is very noble, father, but I think she would be obstinate," replied the Mouse.

"Yes, I am obstinate," boomed the Mountain. "I am not for you."

"Alas, alas!" lamented the Farmer. "Alas, my son! It seems as if we shall never find you a wife! Tell me, Lady Mountain, is there none better than you?"

Then the Mountain groaned, and said, "There is one far better, for though I am obstinate and do not budge, I know of one who will some day destroy me. Dig, dig into my heart. Dig deep!"

The Mouse Bride

Then the Farmer took a spade, and the Mouse dug with his paws, and they made a hole in the Mountain, and were digging when the Mountain groaned again.

"Listen," she begged of them, "oh, listen! Do you not hear?" And they listened.

"I hear nothing," said the Farmer.

"Set your ear to the ground," said the Mountain.

So they set their ears to the ground, and the Mouse's ear was the keener, it was so large and round.

"I hear a sound of scratching!" he cried in excitement.

The Farmer listened again.

"I hear it, too!" he shouted. "Yes, it is most certainly something scratching."

"It is what I told you," sighed the Mountain. "Dig on. It is in my heart."

So the Farmer dug, and the Mouse dug, and the noise from the other side grew louder . . . . scratch, scratch, SCRATCH! And suddenly, the earth broke away before them, and all they could see was a gaping hole, black and deep, reaching into the Mountain's heart.

The Mouse Bride

Together they spoke in whispers into the hole, "Come out, come out! Come out, whoever you are!"

And there stepped forth from the darkness, a lady-mouse!

She wore a cloak of grey silk, her gloves were shell pink, and between her ears was a diadem of dewdrops. And the Farmer would have spoken—would have asked him how he liked her—but the man-mouse held up his paw.

"Do not speak," he said, as if under an enchantment. "This is the lady who must be my wife."

And he gave her his arm, and they walked home slowly together, the Farmer following, a light of wonder in his eyes.

When they reached home the Farmer put his finger to his lips, and his wife nodded.

For she, you remember, knew other things than ploughing.

The Enormous Apple Pie

————————————*————————————

Miss Pussy is cooking a pie, an enormous apple pie. This afternoon all her nieces and nephews are coming to tea, and just imagine how many she has, twenty nephews and nieces; for she comes of a big family and all are married and have children save Miss Pussy herself, which is a pity, for Miss Pussy is good and kind and would make an excellent wife and mother.

So now you can reckon, with so many to eat it, what a very big pie Miss Pussy is to make.

At her side are two great baskets full of golden apples, Bramley Seedlings every one, freshly picked this morning and not a single windfall among them. On the shelf is a tall red canister full of demerara sugar, and her spice box is open on the table scenting the whole kitchen with the sweet smell of nutmeg, clove, cinnamon and allspice, bay leaves, ginger and mace.

First of all Miss Pussy peels and cores the apples with the silver knife her uncle left her, and she throws the first peel over her left shoulder to see who her lover will be; and it falls in the shape of an O, and she smiles to herself at her folly, and anyway, she does not know anyone with a name beginning with O.

Then the apples are sliced up fine into the enormous basin in which she will bake them. She has put a quart jug in the centre to hold up the piecrust, and when the dish is nearly filled to the

The Enormous Apple Pie

brim she sprinkles in the sugar, spoonful after spoonful, pours in enough water to keep it all moist, stirs in cloves, cinnamon and a scattering of almonds, and there is the pie all ready to be covered.

So now she must prepare the pastry, and she goes to the cupboard and pulls out the flour bin, sets her shining copper scales on the table and weighs out the flour, six pounds of it. She pours it into the great bowl she must use for the mixing, and then weighs out the lard, a full three pounds. She mixes this into the flour, sifting it and rubbing it till it is so finely mixed there is not a lump anywhere, a pinch of baking powder, a good squeeze of lemon juice, and then she pours in the water while mixing it all together with a strong wooden spoon; and let me tell you this is hard work, as you may find if you should try. So when the dough is thoroughly mixed Miss Pussy puts on the kettle and sits down for a rest and a nice cup of tea. And when she is rested she sets about rolling out the dough. She sprinkles flour all over the kitchen table, for her pastry board would be far too small for the cover of this pie, and she takes her best glass rolling pin painted with schooners and lovers' knots which Old Tom Cat once gave her after his time at sea in a whaler, and she rolls out the dough till it is even and thin all over the table, then carefully, carefully, so as not to break it, she lifts it on to the top of her pie dish, trims all round it with a pair of scissors, moistens the edge of the dish and the edge of the pastry, presses the two together, and twists all the odd pieces into a twirly decoration to finish it off, with a pastry rose in the centre. Well, I only wish one day you may have so pretty a pie. She remembers to prick little holes in the pastry here and there in a pattern to let the steam out, and then she opens the oven, which she lit early this morning, and she finds it just right, not too hot and not too cold. So in she puts her pie and shuts the door, and sets about cleaning up the kitchen.

The Enormous Apple Pie

This done, she has all the other preparations to make, so she busies herself about the house, making it all neat and tidy, and she does not rest until half-past one, and now the pie should be done. So now she opens the oven door and oh! what a lovely smell of scented apple and crisp brown piecrust. Miss Pussy lifts out the pie and puts it on a table by the window, for on this warm autumn day she thinks it will be nice to eat it cold with junket and a gallon of cream.

Now that every single thing is in order, the house clean, the table set, the sandwiches cut, the cakes and buns she has been making for a week past all set out on her best Coleport dishes, Miss Pussy thinks she will sleep till her guests arrive, for then she will be fresh to entertain them. So Miss Pussy goes up to her bedroom and lies down for a sleep, and leaves her wonderful pie cooling beside the open window.

The Enormous Apple Pie

Oh! Miss Pussy, will you never learn caution? Will you never remember all the rascally people in the world?

No sooner is Miss Pussy asleep than who should come slouch-

ing along the road but old Jackanapes and Snatch, his friend, gossiping of this and that and ready for any kind of mischief.

Snatch is the first to smell the sweet smell of spiced apples,

The Enormous Apple Pie

and nudging Jackanapes he points at the kitchen window framing the pie and then at the window above with the curtain drawn, and no words need to pass between them.

In a moment the two are in the garden and climbing in at the open window.

"Let us not cut the piecrust," whispers Jackanapes, "for we may have a fine joke as well as a good feast."

So very carefully they prise round the edge of the piecrust with a knife till they can lift it off and lay it to one side. And then with all haste they eat up the apples. Think of it, only think of it! Those two rascals alone eat up all the fruit that was to have fed twenty nephews and nieces, to say nothing of Miss Pussy herself; every single bit and the last drop of juice lapped up, and Jackanapes rudely spits the cloves out all over the floor.

Miss Pussy, Miss Pussy, why do you sleep so sound?

This done, Jackanapes whispers to Snatch, and away they skip as fast as they can, and with stomachs so full it is a marvel they can move so nimbly. Down to the marshes they go, and gather there as many great croaking frogs as they can find, and they tie them up in their handkerchiefs, and gathering handfuls of moss away they run back to Miss Pussy.

Miss Pussy's blind is still fast drawn so into the kitchen they go. They lay the moss on the bottom of the dish, and then they lift on the piecrust. Then they take the frogs one by one, and raising the crust just a little they slip the frogs inside it and shut it down again, until every frog is inside, jumping about on the moss and trying to get out.

Jackanapes quickly makes up a paste of flour and water, and fixes down the piecrust to the dish, then he and Snatch run off, leaving the pie by the window just as they had found it.

At half-past three Miss Pussy wakes up, and dresses herself with care, little thinking of what has gone on below while she has slept.

The Enormous Apple Pie

No sooner is she dressed than a carriage rolls up, and out jump her nephews and nieces, all twenty of them, laughing and talking, and hungry for their tea.

"Come in, come in, my dears," says Miss Pussy. "Today I will not keep you waiting, we will eat our tea at once, for I have a huge surprise for you all. Yes, I may say a very big surprise," for Miss Pussy is justly proud of her enormous apple pie.

The nephews and nieces are making such a noise with their chatter that when Miss Pussy goes to bring in the pie she does not hear the croaking that comes from it.

When they see it what a shout comes from her guests, what cries of, "Oh, Aunt Pussy, however did you do it?" and, "Oh, Aunt Pussy, I could eat it all up myself."

And there is so much innocent excitement that no one notices how Jackanapes and Snatch have sidled up to the window and are peeping in to enjoy the consternation they have so unkindly planned.

Miss Pussy takes up the knife and fork.

"Now I will cut the enormous pie," she says, "and the very first piece shall go to the quietest."

At once there is a hush with subdued laughter and whispers from all the nephews and nieces, and now that it is quiet, why, whatever is this?

CROAK CROAK CROAAACK CROAK.

The nieces and nephews all look at each other. Miss Pussy frowns, for she thinks that one of the children is doing it to tease her.

CROAK CROAK CROAK CROAAAK CROAK

And this time it unmistakably comes from inside the pie. Miss Pussy is astonished. She cannot think what it can be. So she quickly thrusts the knife through the crust and cuts out a large slice.

The Enormous Apple Pie

Oh! Mercy on us, what a sight is this!

The great slippery frogs come leaping out in a body, croak-croak-croaking, their golden eyes shining.

Miss Pussy bursts into tears. The nieces shriek. The nephews laugh. "Oh! Aunt Pussy, indeed and indeed this is a great surprise!" For they think it an excellent joke, the humour of small boys being what it is.

But if Jackanapes and Snatch take pleasure from the distress of Miss Pussy, it is not for long.

For now that the frogs are all out of the pie they gather themselves in order around the largest among them, and he, with a great air, draws a fiddle from under his arm, and each of the others produces a musical instrument, till there is a complete orchestra of flutes and strings, and bowing to Miss Pussy, who is dumb with amazement, they strike up a pleasant tune. Motioning to Miss Pussy that she shall follow them, they lead the way back into the pie.

What! Follow a band of frogs into an apple pie! Why, the thing is impossible! But as Miss Pussy and her nieces and nephews crowd round to peer into the pie the opening seems to widen, and quite easily they find themselves walking in a mossy glade, so delightful and charming they think they have found the way to paradise.

The place is enclosed by a semicircle of rocks covered over with moss and ferns, with brilliant flowers growing in among them. A waterfall pours over the highest point into a deep clear pool, from which flows a shallow stream, running over fine sand and pretty coloured stones, and bordered with forget-me-nots and irises.

A willow tree hangs over the farther side in which a willow wren is sitting, singing its song, and though its voice is small and shrill it is distinctly heard above the sound of falling water and the music the frogs are making. For these now are ranged on a ledge of rock, and are quite settled down and ready to play their music for the rest of the afternoon.

Now Miss Pussy sees that a cloth is laid out on the grassy lawn, and on it a feast is spread. And what a feast. Why, even Miss Pussy, for all her generosity and culinary skill, could never have made such a feast as this.

There are nine-and-twenty dishes of sandwiches, egg and cress, cucumber, savoury, and sweet. There are seventeen honeycombs and six big jars of strawberry jam. There are prawns piled high on dishes decorated with seaweed, fresh crab and lobster, and sardines served up in cockle shells.

There are thirty-nine blancmanges, pink and white, and forty jellies of every pretty colour imaginable. There are twenty-five iced cakes each as big as a wedding cake, and forty plates of smaller ones. As for all the dishes of sweets and ice-creams, even if I could tell you all the different kinds there are, you might be tired of hearing it.

And standing in the shallow water in the shadow of a rock to keep them cool are crystal decanters of lemonade, ginger beer, raspberry cordial, cider and cowslip wine.

Since the feast is obviously meant for them, and since the wonders and excitement have done nothing to reduce their appetite, the nephews and nieces quickly range themselves about the cloth and wait for Miss Pussy to bid them begin. When they do they eat and eat and eat, and stint themselves in nothing, but still at the end of it there is so much left that you would think yourself lucky to get the hundredth part of it.

So now they get up and the cloth is cleared away, but they do not see by whom; and then the nieces and nephews scatter about the lovely place, some dancing minuets to the music the frogs are making, others playing games, or climbing among the rocks, others paddling or gathering bunches of flowers to give to Miss Pussy; and she is in a perfect dream of delight sitting in the warm sunshine watching her nieces and nephews enjoying themselves.

But now the willow wren falls silent, a soft mist begins to drift about the glade. The frogs are playing quiet music, and a nightingale is heard.

"Come, children," calls Miss Pussy. "It is getting late. You must finish your games. We must be getting home."

"Oh, Aunt Pussy," cry the nephews and nieces, "must we go so soon? I have never been in such a place before. I should like to stay here for ever."

"Oh! Aunt Pussy, however did you contrive such a wonderful outing?"

But this Miss Pussy cannot answer, for she herself does not know how it happened.

At last she has got them all together, and then the frogs escort them up a little winding path which leads out of the glade; and without quite noticing how it happens Miss Pussy finds herself standing in her little room, her nieces and nephews all around her just as they were when they first peered into the pie.

So is it all a dream? Miss Pussy might almost think so, except that one of her nieces is still wearing a wreath in her hair which she wove by the banks of the stream, and not one of the flowers it is made of is out in Miss Pussy's garden at this time of the year; and while in the glade it was the soft twilight of early June, here in the room it is already dark, for it is late September.

So then Miss Pussy bustles about, dressing the nephews and nieces and wrapping them up for their journey home, for though it was hot enough this afternoon when they came, now it is dark there is a little bite in the air.

Next day comes old Jackanapes.

"Oh, Miss Pussy," he says, "it is noised about in the village that you were taken to an enchanted glade, and there had such a feast as was never heard of before."

The Enormous Apple Pie

Miss Pussy is very pleased to talk of her wonderful outing, and tells old Jackanapes all about it.

"Since you were feasted in the glade," says he, "I suppose all the good things you had prepared yourself are still in the house and still to be eaten?" This is really what he has come for, since he thinks he may get a share in the good things.

But there you are wrong, Mr. Jackanapes, and a good thing, too, since you deserve so badly, for Miss Pussy was up early to-day and packed up all her good things and carried them over to the orphanage, so that others should benefit from the good fortune she has had.

When Jackanapes learns this he will waste his time no longer, but suddenly goes off, and Miss Pussy innocently wonders what has put him out of humour.

Little Red Riding Hood

———————————— * ————————————

In a small village long ago there lived a wood-cutter, his wife and his little daughter. She was a pretty little girl and her mother had made her a beautiful red hood and cloak to match. So she was known to everybody as Little Red Riding Hood.

One day her mother said to her: "Your grandmother is ill, so I want you to go and see her and cheer her up a bit. I am too busy to go myself. I have put some fresh eggs and butter and a loaf of bread and some cakes in that basket, so don't forget to take it with you when you go. But don't loiter on the way and don't speak to anyone you pass."

So Little Red Riding Hood said goodbye to her mother and off she went through the woods in the direction of her grandmother's cottage.

She had not gone very far when she saw a wolf trotting steadily towards her. Before she had much time to think the wolf was in front of her, saying:

"Good morning, my dear. I do admire your lovely red hood. And where might you be going with that heavy basket?"

Red Riding Hood was so pleased with the remark about her hood that she forgot that her mother had warned her not to speak to strangers in the woods.

"I am going to my grandmother's," she said, "she is not very well. And I am taking her some eggs, butter, bread and cakes."

"I see," said the wolf rather thoughtfully. "But if your poor grandmother is ill in bed how will you manage to get in?"

"Oh, I shall first knock three times," replied Red Riding Hood, "and say 'It's me, grandmother!' and then she will tell me how to let myself in."

"Very sensible!" said the wolf. "But I had better be on my way now, I have lots of things to attend to this morning. Goodbye, my dear. I hope grandmother will soon be well again."

So Red Riding Hood continued on her way stopping here and there to pick some pretty flowers for her grandmother. But the cunning wolf waited behind a tree for a little while and then slyly took a short cut to grandmother's cottage. He knocked three times. "Who is there?" came grandmother's rather weak little voice.

"It's me, grandmother," said the wolf, in a little voice just like Red Riding Hood's.

"Well just lift the latch and come straight up," replied grandmother. "I am too weak to get out of bed."

The wolf lifted the latch and was up those stairs in a flash. He swallowed up grandmother, put on her dress and cap and cuddled down deep under the bedclothes.

Just then there came three taps at the door. "Who's there?" said the wolf, in a voice exactly like poor old grandmother's.

"It's me, grandmother," replied Red Riding Hood.

"Just lift the latch and come straight inside," replied the wolf. "I am too weak to get out of bed."

So she opened the door and went up the stairs straight to grandmother's bedside. The wolf's face was just peeping above the bedclothes.

Red Riding Hood put down the basket.

"How are you, grannie?" she asked. "How bright your eyes are this morning!"

Little Red Riding Hood

"All the better to see you with my dear," said the wolf.

"But oh grandmama, how long your nose seems!" said Red Riding Hood.

"All the better to smell you with my dear," said the wolf.

"But oh grandmama, how big your ears are," said Red Riding Hood.

"All the better to hear you with," said the wolf.

"And how huge your teeth are!" said Red Riding Hood.

"All the better to eat you with," said the Wolf, no longer pretending to be grandmother. And with one leap he was out of bed and had gobbled Little Red Riding Hood up.

So now the wolf had both Little Red Riding Hood and grandmother inside his tummy and he felt so heavy and drowsy that he fell sound asleep on the bed, snoring as loudly as anything.

Just then Little Red Riding Hood's father, who as you may remember was a wood-cutter, happened to be passing the cottage and he thought he would pop in and see how grandmother was getting on.

Little Red Riding Hood

He was very surprised to hear the tremendous snoring, which did not at all sound like gentle old grannie.

Into the cottage he went and up the stairs. As soon as he caught sight of the wolf he realized what had happened and he immediately slashed the wolf's tummy right open with his axe. Out sprang Red Riding Hood, none the worse for her experience but just a little startled, and then they gently took out grandmother, suffering from slight shock.

"That was a narrow escape for both of you," said the woodcutter. "Now, Red Riding Hood, go and collect some stones in your basket."

When she returned they filled the wolf's tummy with them so so that when he awoke and tried to spring out of bed the weight dragged him back and he fell down dead.

And now they were all happy again.

"I shall never speak to strangers in the woods again," thought Little Red Riding Hood, "nor loiter on my way."

King Grisly-beard

---- * ----

Princess Liza was very beautiful and extremely clever but she was also so proud and haughty that not one of the princes who came to ask to marry her was good enough for her.

One day the King, her father, held a great feast to which he invited all her suitors—kings, princes, dukes, earls and squires—and they all sat in separate rows according to their rank. Then Princess Liza came into the banqueting-hall and as she walked past each one she made a rather nasty, mocking remark. The first one was too fat: "He's as round as a barrel," she said. The next one was too tall: "What a lamp-post!" she said. The third was too short: "What a dumpling!" she said. The next one was very pale, so she called him "Ghostface". And the fifth one was too red so she called him "Rosynose". The sixth one was rather bent: "Hunchback," scoffed the Princess. And so on she went, making a rather rude joke about each guest. Finally she came to a good, kind king. "Just look at that one," laughed Princess Liza, "his beard is like an old mop. Let's call him Grisly-beard." So the king got the nickname of Grisly-beard.

But the King, Princess Liza's father, was most angry and upset by the way his daughter behaved and he decided that, willing or unwilling, she should marry the first beggar that came to the door.

A few days later a wandering musician came to sing under the palace windows and to beg for a few coppers.

King Grisly-beard

"Let him come in," ordered the King and they brought in a dirty-looking fellow who sang a song before the King and Princess Liza and then begged for a small gift. Then the King said: "You have sung so well that I shall give you my daughter to be your wife." Princess Liza wept and prayed but nothing she said or did could make the King change his mind.

"I have sworn to give you to the first beggar," he said, "and I will keep my word." So they sent for the parson and they were married. And when the ceremony was over the King said, "Now get ready to go; you cannot stay here; you must travel on with your husband."

So the beggar set off with Princess Liza and soon they came to a great wood. It was a really splendid spot with magnificent trees and Princess Liza asked: "Please tell me, whose wood is

King Grisly-beard

this?" "It belongs to King Grisly-beard," answered the beggar. "If you had married him it would have all been yours." "Alas, poor me," sighed the Princess. "I do wish I *had* married King Grisly-beard!"

Soon after they came to a fine meadow. "Whose are these beautiful green meadows?" asked Princess Liza. "They belong to King Grisly-beard," was the reply, "and if you had married him they would have been all yours." "Alas, poor me," sighed the Princess, "I do wish I *had* married him!"

Not long afterwards they came to a great city. "Whose is this splendid city?" asked Princess Liza. "It belongs to King Grisly-beard," came the reply, "and if you had married him it would have been all yours." "Alas, poor me," sighed the Princess, "I do wish I *had* married him!"

"But why do you wish for another husband?" asked the beggar. "Am I not good enough for you?" But Princess Liza did not answer.

A short while after they came to a small cottage.

"What a miserable hovel!" said the Princess. "Whose is this poor little hole?" The beggar replied: "It is your house and it is also my house and that is where we are going to live."

"Where are the servants?" cried the Princess. "We don't need servants," replied her husband, "you must do for yourself whatever needs to be done. So now then, be a good wife, light a fire, boil some water and cook my supper, for I am hungry and tired." But Princess Liza did not know the first thing about making fires or cooking and so the beggar was forced to help her. Between the two of them they somehow managed to prepare a rather scanty meal, which left the Princess very hungry, and then they went to bed. But she had to get up very early next morning, at her husband's call, to clean up the cottage. They went on living like this for two days, though it seemed like two whole years to Princess Liza.

King Grisly-beard

But when they had eaten up all there was in the cottage, the beggar said, "Wife, we simply can't go on like this, spending money and earning nothing. You must learn to weave baskets." So he went out and cut willows and brought them home and she began to weave; but it soon made her fingers very sore. "I can see this work doesn't suit you," said her husband, "perhaps you'd better try some spinning." So the Princess sat down and tried to spin but the threads cut the tender skin of her delicate, white fingers until the blood ran. "Look," said the beggar, "you are good for nothing—you can't weave, you can't spin, you can't cook, you can't do anything. What a fine bargain I've made! I can see I shall have to try to sell some pots and pans so that we can get a few shillings to buy us some food. Yes, you can stand in the market-place and sell them."

"Alas, poor me," sighed Princess Liza, "when I stand in the market-place and the people from my father's court pass by and see me, they will make fun of me!"

But the beggar did not seem to mind about that and said she must work if she did not wish to die of hunger. So off she went to the market and at first things went quite well. For when people saw a beautiful girl selling pots and pans, they hastened to buy from her. She sold all the pots and pans and her husband had to get a fresh lot. But one day a drunken soldier passed by on his horse and drove it against her stall and smashed the pots all to pieces. The Princess wept bitterly. "What will my husband say?" she thought. "Whatever will become of me?" So she ran home, weeping all the way, and told her husband what had happened. "Who would have thought you could be so silly? Fancy getting in the way of a drunken soldier. But anyway, let's have no more of this weeping; dry your tears. I have found you a job as a kitchen-maid at the palace." So a kitchen-maid she became and had to help the cook to do all the dirtiest work. They let her take home some of the meat that was left over and that is what she and her husband lived on.

She had not been working in the palace for very long when she heard that the King's eldest son was going to pass by in a great procession on his way to church to be married. Princess Liza was given some of the rich meat from the wedding feast and she put it in her basket to take home with her.

And now the Princess was standing on the edge of the pavement along with the crowds of people waiting for the prince to come by. Suddenly he appeared, dressed in splendid robes of gold and when he caught sight of the beautiful Liza he stepped forward and took her by the hand. She was so frightened that she tried to run away and in the excitement the cover of her basket fell off and all the meat fell out. Everybody started to laugh and jeer, which made the Princess feel even more ashamed. But the prince would not let go of her hand. Suddenly she managed to break loose and ran towards her home but the prince caught up with her on the doorstep and said: "Don't be afraid of me. I am the beggar-musician who has lived with you in the hut. I brought you there because I loved you. I am also the soldier who overturned your stall in the market-place with my horse. And I am also the man whom you nick-named King Grisly-beard. I have done all this only because I love you and because I wish to cure you of your pride and foolishness. But now, all that is over and done with. You have learnt to be sensible and wise and your old faults are gone. Now it is time to celebrate our wedding feast!"

Then the chamberlains from the Palace came and brought her the most beautiful robes. And her father and his court also came and they were all delighted and amazed at the great change in the Princess. The wedding feast was a grand affair and everybody rejoiced to see Princess Liza now happily united to King Grisly-beard.

Beauty and the Beast

———————————— * ————————————

Long, long ago there lived a very rich man who had three daughters. They were all very beautiful but the youngest was the fairest of them all and she was nicknamed Beauty. This name made her sisters feel very jealous of her. They were not only jealous, however; they were nasty-tempered and lazy while Beauty was always cheerful and smiling. When her two sisters would go out to dances and parties (which was very often), Beauty would go and visit the poor in their cottages and try to help them in their troubles; so she was loved by everyone, rich and poor alike.

Of course, many young men came to the rich man's house to ask for Beauty's hand in marriage, but her answer always was that she felt too young and that, anyway, she wished to be her father's companion and look after him in his old age. But whenever any young man came to ask for the hand of the two sisters *they* refused because they thought the suitors were not rich or important enough for them.

One day their father came home in the evening, called them all together and told them the sad news that he was no longer rich; all his ships had been wrecked at sea and this had left him practically penniless.

Beauty wept when she heard her father's misfortune. "What shall we do now, father dear?" she asked.

Beauty and the Beast

"Alas, my child," he replied, "we must give up our house and go and live in some poor cottage in the country; we must work on a farm with our own bare hands."

"Ah!" said Beauty eagerly, "I can knit, spin and darn. I shall help you all I can, dear father."

But her two sisters said nothing at all. Each of them had secretly made up her mind to marry one of the young men she had once refused and to have nothing at all to do with her father's bad luck. But in this they were greatly mistaken because now that they were poor none of the young men would have anything to do with them.

So very soon the whole family left their rich mansion, sold their costly furniture and went to the country to work in a poor farmhouse. Beauty would get up at six every morning, clean the house, prepare breakfast and decorate the house with flowers to make everything look bright and cheerful. Later on she would cook the dinner so that when her father came home in the evening there would always be a hot meal and a cheerful welcome awaiting him. And all the time she would sing sweet songs. Her sisters gave her no help at all but grew more and more bad-tempered and lazy. They now disliked their sister more than ever and were jealous of her gay and sunny spirit.

Two long years passed by in this way. Then one day a messenger came to the house with the news that one of the rich man's ships had been rescued from the storm at sea and had docked in a port in a far-away land. Beauty helped her father to prepare for his long journey. Before he set out he asked each daughter what gift he should bring back for her. The eldest wished for pearls, the second asked for diamonds and Beauty, the youngest, said: "Father dear, bring me a white rose." So they kissed their father and he bade them good-bye.

He was away for a very long time. Now he was returning home. He had bought the pearls and diamonds for his two

Beauty and the Beast

eldest daughters but he had not been able to find a white rose, although he had looked everywhere and tried with all his might. Some people even laughed at him when he talked of a white rose and said they had never heard of such a thing. This upset him very much, for his youngest daughter was his dearest child. One day as he was coming out of a great park where he had been looking for a white rose he got lost in a wood. It was getting dark and he thought he had better look for somewhere to spend the night because he had heard there were lots of bears in that part of the world. By and by he caught sight of a small light in the distance, so he urged on his tired horse till he came to where it was. He was astonished to find himself outside a magnificent castle. From a massive golden chain by the door hung a twisted golden horn, and this the weary traveller blew. As the beautiful sound echoed through the wood, the heavy old oak doors slowly opened, revealing a vast, wide hall lit up by myriads of golden lamps. No-one appeared, so the man called out:

"If you please, can you kindly give shelter to a weary traveller?"

To his great surprise, two hands moved from behind the door and gently led him down the hall. Thinking of his horse and how tired it must be, the man looked round and saw it being led away to the stables by another pair of shadowy hands. Then he himself was taken upstairs to a large and splendid room where a costly banquet was awaiting him. The two hands served him obediently throughout the meal and when he had finished he was led to a most elegant bedroom. The bed was the most comfortable he had ever slept in and he awoke in the morning to find the sun streaming through the wonderful lace curtains. No sooner was he out of bed than the two hands were there once more, carrying a costly suit of clothes. Then a magnificent bath of warm water appeared from nowhere and so the man bathed and dressed after which he was led down-stairs feeling strong and refreshed. After a most satisfying break-fast the man stood up and said: "Whoever you are that own this castle, please accept my thanks for your wonderful hospita-lity and please let me give you this ring as a token of my grati-tude. And now I must leave, for my three daughters are anxiously waiting for me at home."

On his way to the stables to get his horse, the traveller found himself in the most enchanting garden he had ever set eyes on. Suddenly his gaze fell on a white rose and he immediately thought of the promise he had made to his youngest daughter. "Ah!" he thought, "at last! I am sure the kind owner of this castle will not mind if I pluck just one flower from this splendid garden." And he gently picked the white rose. At that very instant he was startled by a tremendous roar and a fierce lion appeared beside him.

"Whoever dares to steal my roses shall be eaten alive," roared the lion.

"I beg your pardon," said the man respectfully. "I only plucked this one flower as a small present for my daughter. Can I do nothing to save my life?"

"No," replied the Lion, "nothing . . . unless you promise to come back here in a month's time and to bring with you what-ever or whoever meets you first when you return home. If you promise to do this I shall let you go free and let you have this white rose."

The man thought to himself: "Supposing it's my youngest daughter who comes out to meet me first; no, I'd better not promise." Then he thought again: "Well, it will probably be only the dog or cat." So he turned to the lion and said: "I faithfully promise to come back to you in a month's time and to bring with me whoever or whatever comes out to meet me first when I get home."

Beauty and the Beast

So the traveller mounted his horse and set off on his long journey. As he got near his house, whom should he see standing at the door looking into the distance but his dearest youngest daughter. And when she caught sight of her father she gave a cry of joy and came running out to meet him. As she put her arms round his neck and kissed him affectionately, he began to weep.

"Alas, my dearest child," he said, "I have brought you the white rose you asked for, but I have indeed paid a high price for it. I have promised to take you back to a fierce lion and goodness knows what he will do to you." And then he told Beauty all that had happened. But she comforted him and said: "Dear father, do not weep; be of good courage. The promise you have given must be kept. I will go with you to the lion and plead with him and perhaps he will let us both return home safe and sound again."

As the month was drawing to a close it became time for the man to set out with Beauty for the lion's castle. They got everything ready for the long journey and Beauty said good-bye to her sisters. Their horses galloped off and they were soon riding swiftly through the forest which led to the lion's domain. Once again the man blew the twisted golden horn that hung by the door on its heavy chain. As they walked down the wide hall they were greeted by the most beautiful music but not a living creature was to be seen. On entering the dining-room they found a most delicious meal prepared for them and when they had finished the shadowy hands came and removed everything. And then there was a knock at the dining-room door. "Come in," said the man and in walked the lion clad in a handsome red cloak. Beauty almost fainted with fright at first but she soon felt better when the lion sat down opposite her and spoke in the gentlest of tones.

"I am very glad," he began, "that you have kept your

promise. Is this the daughter for whom you plucked the white rose?"

"Yes," answered the man, "and so much does my daughter love me that she insisted on coming with me so that I could keep my promise."

"She will not be sorry she came," said the lion, "for everything in this castle and its gardens will be at her command. But as for you, my good man, tomorrow you must go from here and leave Beauty with me. No harm will come to her, I assure you." He then wished them goodnight and left.

Next morning straight after breakfast Beauty said good-bye to her father and he went home, leaving Beauty all alone with the lion in the great castle. Poor Beauty tried to keep as cheerful as she could and amused herself by walking in the gardens and gathering the white roses.

That evening after dinner, when Beauty was in her room, the lion rapped at her door and asked permission to enter. With a trembling voice she said: "Come in."

"Will you allow me to sit with you?" said the lion as he entered.

"Just as you please," said Beauty as calmly as she could.

"No," said the lion, "for you are mistress here and if you do not like my company you must say so without fear." Beauty was so taken by the lion's polite and gentle manner that she forgot her fears. She asked him to sit down and spoke kindly to him. She tried not to look at his face, though, for it frightened her very much.

The next evening the lion came to visit her once again in her room. This time she was a little less frightened and she spoke to him more kindly than before.

The third evening the lion stayed with her longer than usual and just as he was about to leave he took hold of her hand and said very gently: "Beauty, will you marry me?" She quickly took her hand away and did not answer. The lion gave a deep sigh and left. For the next few days he seemed very sad and did not speak much to Beauty. But not very long after he again asked her to marry him. Beauty replied: "No, dear lion, I cannot marry you, but I will do all I can to make you happy."

"You cannot make me happy unless you marry me," said the lion, "for unless you marry me I shall die."

"Oh please, don't say that!" exclaimed Beauty. "For I am very fond of you. But it is impossible for me to marry you." The lion left her looking more unhappy than ever before.

Now Beauty missed her father a great deal and used to think about him nearly all the time. One day she happened to glance on a strange-looking mirror hanging on the wall of her room and instead of seeing herself she saw her father. The poor man was lying on a bed looking terribly pale and ill while in the room next door were her two sisters trying on their fine dresses. At this sight Beauty wept bitterly and when the lion came to her room a little later he could see how very upset she was. She told him what she had seen and said she wished to go home to look after her father in his sickness. Then the lion said: "Beauty, if I let you go to nurse your father, will you promise to come back to me when he is well?" Beauty gave him her promise. The lion gave her an especially beautiful white rose, saying:

"With this rose you can wish yourself wherever you please to be; but do not forget to keep your promise to come back to me." Then he left her.

Beauty immediately wished herself in her father's cottage and found herself outside the door. Full of joy, she ran into the house and up to her father's bedroom. He was so overjoyed to see her that he immediately began to feel a little better.

The two sisters were very annoyed by their younger sister's return and very jealous to see her so finely dressed. Beauty told them all about the lion's castle and how she had promised to return to him by a certain day. The sisters got more and more jealous as they listened to her story and in the end they made up their minds to try their best to stop her from getting back to the castle.

"Why should this young miss be better off than we are?" said the eldest to the youngest. "Let us make her break her promise to the lion. That will make him so angry with her that he might do something terrible to her when she does get there."

"That is an excellent idea," said the other sister, who was equally spiteful and cruel. "We shall delay her here for as long as we can."

From then on they pretended to be very loving to Beauty and treated her very affectionately. The day before she was due to leave they stole the white rose which the lion had given to Beauty and wished themselves in some grand palace. But it did not work. Instead of being carried away as they expected, they saw the beautiful white rose wither and fade in front of their very eyes. They were so frightened that they threw the rose into a corner and hid themselves.

Beauty was very distressed by the loss of her rose and looked everywhere for it. At last she happened to walk into her sisters' room and saw the rose lying withered in the corner. She wept bitterly, but as soon as she picked it up it recovered all its freshness and loveliness. She now realized that she had broken her promise to the lion, so she went and said good-bye to her father and wished herself in the lion's castle. She was there in an instant and found everything as she had left it except for one thing. The enchanting music which used to greet her whenever she entered the castle was now hushed. A heavy, gloomy silence hung depressingly over everything. Beauty herself felt very sad but she did not know why. When she went up to her room that evening she waited for the lion as usual but no lion appeared. "Perhaps he is very angry with me," she thought, "because I did not keep my promise. Or perhaps he has died, as he said he would if I did not marry him." At this terrible thought Beauty grew very frightened and spent a miserable and sleepless night. The next morning she went hurrying through every room in the castle looking for the lion. But he was nowhere to be seen. Then she walked slowly out into the garden. "If I had married him," she thought, "I might have saved his life. I do wish I could see him just once more." At that very moment she looked down at

a plot of grass and saw the poor lion lying there, as if dead. Beauty knelt down by his side and took hold of his paw. The lion opened his eyes and said: "Beauty, you forgot your promise, and so I must die."

"No, dear lion," she cried, "you shall not die. What can I do to save your life?"

"Will you marry me?" he asked.

"Yes," replied Beauty.

No sooner had she said this magic word than the lion disappeared and there before her stood a handsome Prince. He told her how a wicked magician had changed him into a lion and told him that he never would become his real self again until a beautiful girl would agree to marry him. But then a good fairy had given him the white rose which, she said, would one day help to break the magician's wicked spell.

The Prince led Beauty into the castle, which was now full of courtiers. He then sent a carriage and horses to fetch Beauty's father. Of course, the Prince asked him to allow Beauty to become his wife and, of course, he gladly gave his consent. There was a great wedding-feast (to which the two sisters were too jealous to come, although Beauty had kindly invited them) and the young couple lived happily together for many, many years.

Tim Rabbit's Umbrella

————————————————*————————————————

One morning, when Tim Rabbit put his head out of the door, it was raining. Now, every rabbit likes a little rain, for it fills the cups of the grasses with sweet water, and refreshes and cools hot tired little feet, but this was a lot of rain. It was as if a giant were throwing buckets and buckets of water out of the sky, and all the rain seemed to be pouring into Tim's garden and the meadows across the common.

Tim's heart sank. He had intended to go exploring with Sam Hare that day, and now he knew Mrs. Hare wouldn't let Sam go out at all. He didn't think his mother would allow him to go, either, for the heavy rain would soak him to the skin, and make him like a miserable rat. Tim didn't like rats, and he didn't like rain when it came down like this, in torrents.

As he stared sadly at the downpour he heard tiny footsteps. Flip flop! Flip flop! they came, paddling along a little path on the common, past the door of Tim's house, towards the lily-pond. It was Emily Duck in her white dress and bonnet.

"Good morning, Tim Rabbit," she called in a friendly way as she caught sight of the sad little nose poking through the doorway.

"Bad morning, Emily," returned Tim. "It's very rainy."

"Yes, delightfully rainy. Just the weather I love," answered the duck, shaking her waterproof skirts, and patting her little feather bonnet with pride.

Tim Rabbit's Umbrella

Tim looked at her enviously.

"Where are you going?" he asked, although he knew quite well. He wanted to be sure, and to have a little chat on a wet morning.

"To the pond for my breakfast, and then to the stream for my morning swim," said Emily gaily. "Would you like to come with me?"

Tim stared. "Emily," said he, in a hesitating manner, for he didn't want to put rude questions to a sedate old bird like Emily. "Will you tell me something? Will you tell me why you don't get wet?"

"That's simple enough," laughed the duck. "It's because I wear a mackintosh dress. All my family wear mackintoshes, and they can go out in any weather. The rain simply rolls off," and she shook her feathers to show the little round glassy drops, tumbling to the ground.

"I wish I had one, too," said Tim, mournfully.

"Well, goodbye! I must be off! My breakfast is waiting for me in the pond. Such a delicious breakfast!" She snapped her beak in anticipation as she waddled off across the watery common.

Tim gazed after her, and then he gingerly stepped out from the doorway, but the rain beat down and soaked his coat and trousers, so he retreated indoors till the sun came out.

Still thinking of Emily Duck he trotted through the wet grass to the stream. There she was, with a company of sisters and cousins, and her brother, handsome Dick Drake, in his bright green mackintosh coat and trousers. How happy they were, standing on their heads, and diving in the water!

As Tim watched the merry company, it began to rain again, so he crept under the shelter of a low thorn-bush and waited.

Clump! clump! clumperty clump! sounded on the bridge over the stream. Little John, from the farm, stamped across, with his bag on his back, going to school. He carried a big umbrella, and all the rain bounced on the top and then bounced off. He wore a black mackintosh, and a pair of Wellingtons. Tim Rabbit peeped at the rosy face and the big brown eyes under the umbrella, and John peered back at the bright eyes of the rabbit.

"Hello, Bunny!" said John. "Would you like to come under my 'brella?"

Tim Rabbit didn't answer. He didn't want to go to school, but he admired the umbrella, and the way it kept John dry. He thought and he thought, as he sat sheltering under the bush. He had seen umbrellas growing somewhere. Where was it? Then he remembered. It was in the pasture, the field called Daisy Spot, with its hedge of roses and honey-suckle. That's where umbrellas grew! He wouldn't bother about a mackintosh. He would be clever like John at the farm. He would have an umbrella!

As soon as the rain ceased he said good-bye to the ducks and went away to seek for umbrellas. Soon he found a very large one, with a white silken cover on the top, and pale pink frills underneath. So sweet it smelled, and so pearly white it looked in the green grass, Tim sat by it for a while before he ventured to pick it! Surely it belonged to the Fairy Queen herself, her State Umbrella, for her Coronation Day!

Then he nipped off the stalk close to the ground, and held the giant mushroom proudly over his head. He twirled it, and twisted it, and stared up at the pretty delicate ribs above him, and the satiny skin on the stalk.

"Look at Tim Rabbit under a mushroom," whistled a shrill mocking voice, and there was his old enemy, the jay.

"It's an umbrella," answered Tim, and he twiddled it in the face of Jim Jay.

"What's it for?" asked Jim, curiously.

"To keep off the rain," said Tim, and Jim Jay laughed his

loud screaming laugh which echoed through the woods, and flew away.

"I wish it would rain now," said Tim to himself. "I should like to show them all." He sat down and waited, whilst a black cloud rolled over the sky. The trees shivered, and down came the rain once more.

Then Tim Rabbit walked happily and proudly across the fields, carrying the big mushroom over his head, sheltering his body from the wet. He could only walk slowly, but that didn't matter—more animals could see and admire the way he turned his umbrella to meet the rain.

"Look at Tim, out in all this rain," cried his small cousin, popping her head out of a hole. "He's carrying a mushroom. Isn't he clever?"

"Umbrella," corrected Tim as he went by.

"Quick! Look at Tim Rabbit, walking under a mushroom," exclaimed the hedgehog to his brother, under the hedge.

"Umbrella," called Tim, waving a paw, and nearly dropping the mushroom.

"Goodness! Whatever's this? A mushroom out walking? Just what I want," and a paw stretched out and grabbed Tim's umbrella.

"My umbrella! Please!" said Tim fiercely, and the old rabbit, muttering, "Sorry, my mistake," scurried off in the rain.

"If that isn't my nephew Tim, bringing me a fine mushroom for my dinner! What a kind rabbit he is to come out in all this rain," said Aunt Eliza, peering from her door at the sound of the tiny footsteps.

"Umbrella!" grunted Tim, walking rapidly past.

"It's a bitter disappointment," grumbled Aunt Eliza. "I wanted a mushroom on this wet day. It is good for rheumatism."

"It's a bitter umbrella," called Tim, to comfort her, but she shut the door, and sat down to cry.

Tim Rabbit's Umbrella

"Well done, Tim Rabbit," said Emily Duck, when she saw Tim walking across the bridge on his way home. "It's as good as John's, and even better, for his umbrella is made of black cotton, and yours is white silk!"

"She knows!" said Tim to himself. "She knows this is an umbrella. She is the only person with any sense."

At last he got home, tired and hungry, but extremely happy, for he was dry as a duck, and proud as a peacock.

Mrs. Rabbit stood at the door, waiting for him.

"Tim," she cried, "I wondered where you were. Are you very wet? What are you carrying?"

"My umbrella. A present for you, Mother," said Tim putting the mushroom on the floor.

"Hum! It would just do for a table," said Mrs. Rabbit, looking at it. "I never saw such a big mushroom, Tim."

"Umbrella," corrected Tim, once more.

"I think we will have some fried umbrella for supper," said Mrs. Rabbit, calmly, and she put the frying-pan on the fire and sat down to peel part of the mushroom.

Soon there was a delicious smell and a sizzling and spluttering in the pan. Tim and his parents ate fried umbrella for a whole week. From the satiny skin of the mushroom Mrs. Rabbit made a little pair of bedroom slippers, which Tim wears to this day.

So, whenever it rains, all that Tim has to do is to go to the meadow for a mushroom, and then he can walk round and visit his friends who sit at home.

Tom Tit Tot

————————————————*————————————————

Once upon a time a woman put five pies into the oven to bake but forgot to take them out in time. The crusts were so hard you couldn't get your teeth into them.

"Ah well, never mind," she said to her daughter Joan, "we'll just put them on the shelf and they'll soon come again."

What she meant was that in time they would become soft enough to be eaten. But Joan didn't understand. She thought they really would come again.

"Well, if they really will come back again I may as well eat these." So she cut off the hard crusty pieces with a sharp knife and ate all five of the pies.

At supper time her mother said: "Joan, go and get two or three of those pies from the shelf." So Joan went and looked but of course they weren't there.

"They haven't come again, mother, as you said, so we can't have them for supper."

"Not come yet?" asked her mother. "Just bring one along and let me have a look."

"I can't, mother," replied Joan, "I ate them all up and not a single one has come again."

"What!" exclaimed her mother. "You mean to say you ate all those pies. What an appetite you must have!"

Anyway that was that. There were no pies for supper that

evening, so the mother went and sat by her spinning-wheel in the doorway and began spinning. And as she spun she sang to herself:

> "*My daughter's eaten five pies today*
> *Five pies today*
> *Five pies today*
> *My daughter's eaten five pies today*
> *What a* . . . . "

Just at that moment the King happened to be coming down the street and he said to the woman:

"What were those words you were singing, my good woman? I couldn't quite catch them."

Well, as you may imagine, the woman didn't like to tell the King the real words because that would make her daughter out to be a very greedy girl. So she thought very quickly and said with a curtsey:

> "*My daughter has spun five skeins today*
> *Five skeins today*
> *Five skeins today*
> *My daughter has spun five skeins today*
> *And* . . . . . "

"Aha!" said the King with some astonishment. "You have indeed got a clever daughter. I should like to see her."

The woman called Joan to the door and Joan made a deep curtsey. The King looked at her and said:

"I am looking for a wife. You seem to be the right kind of girl. How would you like to marry me and become Queen?"

"Very much indeed," replied Joan with another deep curtsey.

"Well then," said the King, "you shall be my wife and become Queen of the land. And for eleven months of the year you may have all the clothes you want, all the money you need, all the food you desire and all the friends you like. But for the twelfth month of the year you must spin me FIVE SKEINS EVERY DAY."

"That suits us fine, Your Majesty," replied the woman, for she thought they would manage it somehow, and anyway by the time the twelfth month came the King would have forgotten all about it.

So there was a magnificent wedding and Joan became Queen and lived at the Palace. For eleven months she wore the most splendid clothes and invited all her friends. She had all her favourite dishes and spent ever so much money.

When the last day of the eleventh month came the King took Joan up to a room she had never seen before on the top floor of the palace. There was nothing in the room except a bare spinning wheel, a stool, a table and a bed.

"Now," said the King. "This is where you must stay for the whole of the next month. Every morning I will bring you your breakfast and some flax and every evening I will bring you your supper and take away the five skeins you have spun. And if you haven't spun five skeins by the evening . . . BEWARE! something TERRIBLE will happen to you."

Poor Joan was so frightened she burst out crying, but the King went away without saying another word.

She cried and cried, for she knew the King would soon find out that she could not spin, for she had never learnt how to use a spinning wheel.

All of a sudden, amidst her tears, she heard a tiny little rap at the door. "Come in!" sobbed Joan and in came a small black creature, thin and rather long, with shining eyes, pointed ears and a big tail.

"And what may be the matter with you!" asked the creature, twitching his ears.

"It won't do me any good if I tell," said Joan.

"Maybe it will and maybe it won't," said the black thing, "but tell me all the same."

So Joan fetched a deep sigh and told him all about the pies "not coming again", about her marrying the King, about the five skeins, and with many a choking sob she told him that something terrible would happen if she didn't spin five skeins.

"Well, just you listen to me," said the black thin creature. "When you get the flax each morning I will come and take it away, and in the evening I will bring it back spun into five skeins just as the King wants it."

"And what do I have to do for all this?" asked Joan suspiciously. The little black creature's eyes gleamed and his ears twitched furiously.

"Every day," he said, "I shall give you three guesses and you must guess my name. If you haven't guessed it by the end of the month, I shall have you for myself."

"All right," said Joan, "that's a bargain."

And with a whisk of his tail the black thing was gone.

The next day in came the King with the flax and breakfast. "Get on with your spinning," he said, "for you know what will happen tonight if it isn't spun into five skeins."

Out he went and in seconds there was a tiny rap at the door and when Joan opened it, sure enough there stood the little black thing. Without a word he went and picked up the flax and was off again. That same evening, with the same little rap, he was back again with the spun skeins.

"Now," he says, twitching his ears. "What's my name?"

"Dick," she said.

"W-R-O-N-G," he said, exactly like a gong.

"Tom," she said.

"W-R-O-N-G," he gonged.

"Jack," she said.

"W-R-O-N-G," he gonged again. And with a whisk of his tail he was off.

Then in came the King.

"Ah," said he, "I see you have done your job. You are safe for tonight." And he left.

And so every day afterwards, breakfast and flax were brought in by the King and every day, morning and evening, the little black imp would come to take the flax away and bring it back spun into five skeins. And every day the black imp asked Joan to guess his name. But to every single name that she guessed he said, "W-R-O-N-G" exactly like a gong, because she couldn't guess it right.

And now on the last but one day, Joan was getting desperate. She thought she would try names from the Bible.

"Joseph."

"W-R-O-N-G."

"Abraham!"

"W-R-O-N-G."

"Moses."

"W-R-O-N-G."

And off he went again with a whisk of his tail and twitching his ears more furiously than ever.

And now in came the King and when he saw the spun skeins he looked very pleased and said, "You have done very well and I'm sure that you'll have the last five skeins all spun tomorrow evening. So to celebrate I'm going to join you for supper."

So another stool was brought in for the King and they had a right royal meal and Joan enjoyed it because her husband looked so pleased and talked so gaily to her. "Do you know what, my dear," the King said, "a most amusing thing happened to me this morning when I was out hunting. We got to the edge of a little forest where I had never been before and my horse stopped dead, right on the brink of an old chalk pit. At the bottom of this pit I could see a funny little black creature with a twirling tail sitting on a stool and spinning furiously away at a tiny spinning wheel. It was singing a funny little song with curious words:

> *"Nimmy Nimmy Not,*
> *My name is TOM TIT TOT."*

And the King laughed heartily. Joan's heart beat fast because she guessed that this was her little imp, but she didn't say a word. But when the King had left she kept saying the little jingle over and over to herself, so that she shouldn't forget the little black imp's name.

> *"Nimmy Nimmy Not,*
> *My name is TOM TIT TOT."*

When the next night came the creature was back as usual with the five skeins, his little eyes shining more brightly and his ears twitching more fiercely than ever.

"What is my name?" he asked.

Joan tried to look very scared, "Is it Jackanapes?"

"W-R-O-N-G."

"Is it Plonkadoodle?"

"W-R-O-N-G" and the little black thing came closer and closer.

Then Joan pointed her finger at him and said with a little laugh:

> *"Nimmy Nimmy Not*
> *Your name is TOM TIT TOT!"*

And when the creature heard those words it gave a tremendous shriek and whisking its tail violently it flew out of the window and that was the end of that. For a bargain's a bargain. And then the King came to take Queen Joan downstairs to feast with him in the Palace Hall and they lived happily ever after.

The Six Servants

———————————————*———————————————

L ong, long ago many handsome young princes came to the
palace of a beautiful princess to try to win her hand in
marriage.

But not a single one of them had any luck and this was all
because of the princess's mother, a wicked, ugly queen. For she
was not only a queen but a nasty witch and she could weave all
sorts of terrible spells and charms. Every time one of these
princes came to the palace the witch-queen would send for him
and say: "Before you can win my daughter's hand there are three
jobs you must do. If you can do them, well and good, you may
marry the princess. But if not . . . ." And her face would take
on a frightening expression. And she would make these jobs so un-
believably difficult that no prince could ever hope to do them.

Several years passed like this and the princess began to
wonder why none of these handsome, strong young princes
could ever win her for his wife.

Now, far away, in another palace lived a particularly dashing
young prince. He had heard about the princess and her ugly
mother and he decided he would go and see whether he could
do these difficult tasks and so marry the princess. But the king,
his father, said: "No, my son, you must not go to that wicked
witch-queen's palace. You may never return alive. Have you
not heard the dreadful tales about her?"

"Please, father, do let me try!" pleaded the prince.

But the king refused again and again.

The prince became very sad and soon fell ill. He went to bed and nothing would cheer him up. For many months he lay in bed, pale and hardly eating anything. At last his father came to his bedside and said: "Very well, my son, I shall allow you to go to the witch-queen's palace. But take great care."

At these words the prince cheered up immediately and was soon well and strong again. One morning he galloped off on his favourite horse and all the ladies and gentlemen of the Court waved good-bye and good luck.

After he had ridden many miles he suddenly saw an enormous hill stuck right in the middle of a heath. Puzzled, he trotted up and found it was not a hill but an enormous fat man lying on his back gazing up at the sky.

"Ho, ho!" laughed the fat man, "Can I be of any service to Your Highness?"

"Well, I don't think you could be of much use to me," said the prince.

"Yes, I could," replied the man. "Do you know, when I

spread myself out I am five hundred times as big as I am now."

"Very well," said the prince, "in that case I am well able to use a fellow like you. Thank you very much."

So they both travelled on together until, soon after, they saw an enormous pair of feet pointing up from the ground. They could not see the legs until they got right beside the feet and even then they could not see where the legs ended because they seemed to go on and on and on. First they came to the calves of the legs, then a long while later to the knees and then, much later, to the thighs. Finally, they reached the body and then they came to the man's head and face.

"Hello!" said the face. "Can I be of any help to you? When I am stretched to my full length I am ten thousand times as long as I am now."

"Yes, thank you," said the prince. "I certainly think you will be able to help me."

And so now the prince, the fat man and the long man all travelled on together. Very soon they came to a man with an enormously long, thin, neck. He kept twisting his neck this way and that and staring out of his crystal-clear eyes which gave forth great beams of light.

"What on earth are you staring at, my good fellow?" asked the prince.

"I'm staring at everything," said Sparkle-Eyes. "There's nothing I can't see. Every mountain, every valley, every river, every cottage. By the way, can I be of any help to you?"

"Yes, I should think so, indeed," said the prince. "Thank you very much."

And so now there were four of them and they all travelled on together.

Not very long after they saw a man bending down with his ear to the ground.

"And what may you be listening to, my good man?" asked the prince.

"Well my ears are extra large, as you can see," replied the man. "There's nothing I can't hear. Even what the daisies are whispering to one another through the grass. So I'm just listening. Can I help you in any way?"

"You certainly can," said the prince. "Thank you very much."

And so now they were five and they all continued their journey together.

Shortly afterwards they met a man whose eyes were bandaged.

"What is the matter, my good fellow?" asked the prince. "Have you got bad eyes?"

"On the contrary," answered the man. "I have very good eyes, very strong eyes. So strong, in fact, that whatever they look at breaks into a million pieces. Can I be of any help to you?"

"You certainly can," replied the prince. "Thank you very much."

And so Blindfold came along with them, making six in all.

They had not gone very far when they came upon a man sitting at the edge of the wood, all hunched up and swathed in lots of scarves and shawls. Although it was a very warm day, with the sun blazing down, this man was still shivering with cold.

"What ails you, my good fellow?" asked the prince. "Have you a fever?"

"No," replied the man. "I am not ill really. It is just that the hot weather makes me feel cold. The hotter the weather, the chillier I feel. Brrrr! But perhaps I can help you in some way."

"Yes, I think you could," replied the prince. "Come along and join us and thank you very much indeed."

And so now the prince had six servants, the Fat Man, the Long-Legged One, Sparkle-Eyes, Big-Ears, Blindfold and Chilly-One. And they all went along together, behind the prince.

The Six Servants

After a few days' travel they reached the land of the witch-queen. The prince left his six faithful servants at an inn and went along alone to the palace. He was summoned before the queen and he said:

"I wish to wed the beautiful princess and am willing to do any task you set for me."

"Fine, fine!" said the queen. "A handsome young man like you should have no difficulty at all"—all the time thinking in her wicked heart that he would fail as all the many others had failed before him.

"Well," said the prince. "What's my first task to be?"

"Well," replied the queen, "I have three tasks for you. To win the hand of the princess you must do them all. And if you fail in any one—well, my lad, that will be the end of you, I'm afraid.

"Here is your first task:

"At the bottom of the Red Sea there's a ring. You must bring it to me by midday today."

The prince bowed and walked off to the inn where his six faithful servants were staying.

"The witch-queen wants the ring that's lying at the bottom of the Red Sea," he told them. "It's no easy task, but we shall get it."

"Of course we will," said Sparkle-Eyes. "Let me have a look." And stretching his long thin neck as far as it would go he stared far, far into the distance, till the beams from his eyes shone right down into the bottom of the Red Sea.

"I can see it," he cried. "It's right in the middle, just hanging on the ledge of a rock." Then the Long-Legged One took them all on his back and with a few giant strides he had carried them to the banks of the Red Sea. Now it was the Fat Man's turn. He blew and blew until he was five hundred times as fat as before. Then he knelt down by the water and drank and drank until not one drop of the Red Sea was left. And there on a ledge lay the ring. The Long-Legged One leaned over and seized it, handed it to the prince, then put all the servants and the prince on his back and carried them back to the inn.

The prince then rode to the palace and presented the ring to the queen. She was too disappointed to speak, and mumbled: "Yes, yes, that's the ring, that's the ring. Easy job, easy job. Now the second task. Are you ready?"

"Yes," said the Prince.

"Well," she said, "in my fields you will find three hundred plump cows. By sunset tonight you must eat every single one—horns, tail, hooves and everything. Then you must go to my wine cellar and drink up five hundred bottles of red wine—all by sunset. Off you go, my lad. You can invite one guest if you like," she added with an ugly grin, "but only one—just to keep you company."

Off went the prince back to the inn. When he got there he said to the Fat Man, "I've got a treat for you, my good fellow. Today you shall be my guest at the greatest banquet of your life."

When the Fat Man saw the three hundred cows and the five hundred bottles of wine he blew himself out until he was five hundred times as fat as he had been. He quickly gobbled up all the oxen, tail, horns, hooves and everything and then just as quickly drank every drop of the five hundred bottles of wine.

"Not a bad meal," he said to the prince. "Thank you very much." Then, feeling rather drowsy, he gave a mighty yawn and fell fast asleep.

When the witch-queen saw that the second task was done she found it hard to hide her fury. However, she put on a sort of crooked smile and said, "Very good. And now for the third task. Are you ready?"

"Ready, Madam," said the prince. "What is it to be?"

The Six Servants

"Listen," said the witch-queen. "Tonight you must sit with the princess and put your arm round her shoulder. You must not fall asleep and she must not leave you all night. I shall come and see you at midnight and if she isn't there with you, then it's all over with you, my lad."

"Don't worry, Madam," said the prince. "I shall keep wide awake and hold her tight." But secretly he thought to himself that the witch-queen had some cunning trick up her sleeve and so he went back to the inn and told them that they must all keep watch with him that night.

In the evening the queen drove up to the inn with the princess. She led the prince and princess to a large room, sat them on a bench and placed the prince's arm around the princess's shoulder. Then she left them. As soon as she was out of sight the Long-Legged One lay down on the floor and curled himself round the bench so that the princess could not get away. The Fat Man stood by the door and the four others all stood in readiness in case anything unexpected should happen. Well, the night wore on and the young couple sat there happily. But one hour before midnight the witch-queen cast a spell over them all and in a moment the prince fell fast asleep and so did the Fat Man and the Long-Legged one and Sparkle-Eyes and Big-Ears and Blindfold and Chilly-One. Luckily, however, the spell was not quite strong enough, for a quarter of an hour before midnight the spell wore off and they all woke up. But, alas, the princess was gone!

"Good Heavens!" exclaimed the prince rather alarmed. What on earth am I to do now? The witch-queen has caught me."

"Wait a moment," said Big-Ears, listening carefully, "I think I can hear someone crying. Yes, yes, it's the princess! She is crying. Have a look, Sparkle-Eyes."

And Sparkle-Eyes took a good, long look. About five hundred

miles long. The bright beams from his eyes shone right across
from east to west.

"I can see her," he said, "she's sitting on a rock. Come on,
Long-Legs, go and fetch her!"

"Certainly," said Long-Legs, "but I shall need the help of
Blindfold. Come along. I'll take you on my shoulders." And off
he started, stretching his legs out to their full length. In a few
steps he was standing right beside the rock. The princess sat
crying deep down inside it. Blindfold lifted the bandage from,
his eyes, *just for one second*, and the rock shattered into a thousand
pieces. Then the Long-Legged One lifted the princess out, quite
unhurt. She was very happy to be free. And then in three or
four giant strides all three of them were back at the inn once
more—but only just in time. For the prince had hardly put his
arm round the princess's shoulder when it struck midnight and
in came the witch-queen. You can imagine her rage when she
saw the princess there, perfectly safe next to the Prince. But she
hadn't finished her mischief yet. Her wicked brain started to
think out all sorts of nasty plans. She bent down as if to kiss her
daughter but instead whispered something in her ear. The
princess turned pale—for she was bound to obey her mother's
command.

"Prince," she said, "you have won my hand, for you have
completed all three tasks, but I have not given *my* consent yet,
have I?"

"No," said the prince. "You have not. What must I do in
order to have it?"

The witch-queen bent down and quickly whispered something else in her daughter's ear—while again pretending to kiss
her. And the poor princess said to the prince, in a rather trembling voice:

"A big bonfire will be made here right away. If you can find
someone to sit right in the middle of it, I will marry you."

The Six Servants

The witch-queen grinned, for she was certain she had the prince caught now. She thought the prince would have to sit on the bonfire himself—for who would be willing to get burnt for his sake? But then, she did not know about Chilly-One. The servants took Chilly-One by the hands and gently pulled him forward, saying, "Go on, Chilly-One, it's your turn to help the Prince now." For Chilly-One, you will remember, got colder and colder the hotter it became.

The bonfire was already blazing away fiercely. Chilly-One pulled his scarves and shawls around him and jumped right into the middle of the bonfire. All the others moved away, for it gave out a mighty heat. The bonfire went on burning for many days. At last, when the last flames were dying away, they all came along to see what had happened. And there stood Chilly-One shaking and shivering with cold and his teeth chattering with a great clatter. "Th-th-th-ank H-h-heavens th-thats over," he kept saying. "I couldn't have stood it much longer."

The prince and the servants were delighted. But when the witch-queen saw what had happened and realized that all her plans had come to nothing she thought she had better run away before anyone could catch her. But just as she was about to escape Blindfold lifted his bandage for one second and the queen was shattered into a thousand pieces. And that was the end of that awful creature.

And so now the princess was free to marry the handsome Prince. He rode away with her to his father's palace, where they got married and lived happily ever after. As for the faithful servants, he did not forget them either. He built them a splendid house where they all lived together in peace and friendship and helped the prince whenever he needed them.

Jack and the Beanstalk

———————————*———————————

There was once a widow who lived with her son Jack in a little cottage. All they had was a cow, which gave them milk, and a little patch of garden in which they grew vegetables. Some of the milk Jack churned into butter and he would take this to sell in the market, together with the vegetables they grew. So although they were very poor they were quite happy, but Jack often wished he could earn a little more money so that he could make life more easy and comfortable for his mother. But things got worse instead of better. For one morning when Jack went to milk the cow, no milk came. And the same thing happened the next morning and the morning after. And when Jack's mother went to pick the vegetables she found they were dying because the earth had grown dry and hard.

"Look here, Jack," said his mother, "I think we had better sell the cow; we simply must have some money to buy food."

"Righto!" said Jack. "I will take her to market tomorrow morning."

So next day Jack got up very early and set off for the market.

He hadn't gone far when he met an old man.

"Good morning, Jack," said the old man, "and where may you be going with that cow?"

Jack wondered how the old man knew his name, for he had

never seen him before, but he answered politely, "I am taking her to market to sell, for she doesn't give any milk and my mother and I have nothing to live on."

"How about selling her to me?" asked the old man. "Very likely you won't get much money for her at the market."

"I'd be glad to, sir," said Jack, "if you will give me a fair price," thinking how nice it would be if he didn't have to drag all that long way to market.

The old man put his hand into his pocket and pulled out a handful of beans.

"Here you are," he said, "I'll give you these in exchange for your cow."

Jack thought the old man must be a bit simple and said as politely as he could: "Oh no, sir, I think I could get more for it at the market. I'd better be getting along."

"Wait a moment, my boy," said the old man. "These are no ordinary beans, you know, you just have to plant them and they'll shoot right up to the sky. Yes, up to the sky. Over night."

"Ah, magic beans!" thought Jack. "That would be nice." But he still hesitated.

"I'll tell you what," said the old man. "If they don't work, I'll give you your cow back."

Well, that sounded fair enough to Jack, so he took the beans, handed the cow over to the old man and made off for home.

"Well, Jack," said his mother. "How much did you get for her?"

Jack placed his beans on the table. "There," he said, "that's what I got for her."

His mother thought he was joking.

"No, Mother," said Jack. "An old man gave me them. But don't worry, Mother, they are magic beans. Just wait and see what will happen to them by tomorrow morning."

"Stuff and nonsense!" said the poor widow angrily. "Off to

bed with you," and she flung the beans out of the window into the garden.

Jack felt very sorry to see his mother so upset. He also remembered that he had forgotten to ask the old man where he lived, so he could never get their cow back even if the beans didn't turn out to be magic. Finally, he fell asleep. He awoke in the morning to the singing of the birds but was surprised to notice how dark it seemed in his bedroom which was usually so bright.

He ran to the window and saw that there were enormous great leaves pressed up against it from an enormous great beanstalk which was growing up from the garden right into the sky. He dressed hurriedly, ran down into the garden and began to climb up the beanstalk. It was easy to climb, and he went up and up until he got to the very top, right above the clouds. And there he found himself in a pleasant country of green fields and meadows and across one of these fields there was an inviting-looking path leading to a great gleaming castle.

"That looks very interesting," thought Jack and he started walking along the path. It took him much longer than he expected to reach the castle but when he got quite close he met a woman carrying a milk-pail on her head.

"And where are you going, Jack, may I ask?" (Jack thought it odd that she knew his name.) "Not to the castle, I hope. There is a giant living there, he loves eating little boys. He'll be wanting his supper soon and if he gets a sniff of you he'll gobble you up in seconds. So you'd better get back where you came from before he comes home."

But Jack felt so tired from his walk that he begged the woman to give him a slice of bread and a drink of water. She took him into her kitchen and gave him some bread and a mug of milk. He had just about finished when he heard a tremendous banging of giant footsteps and the whole castle seemed to tremble.

Jack and the Beanstalk

"Heavens above! That's the giant," cried the woman, and she pushed Jack into her oven and slammed the door on him just in the nick of time. For in came the giant carrying six dead goats and three calves over his shoulder.

"Prepare these for my supper, woman," he bawled, "I'm hungry." Then he looked round suspiciously and began to sniff. Jack heard him shout:

> *"Fee foh fi fum*
> *I smell the blood of an Englishman.*
> *Be he alive or be he dead*
> *I'll grind his bones to make my bread."*

"He must mean me," thought Jack, scared.
But then he heard the woman saying, "Stuff and nonsense.

Jack and the Beanstalk

It's just your imagination. Take your boots off and have a rest while I prepare your supper."

Shortly after Jack could hear the giant munching great chunks of meat and gulping down great draughts of some drink or other.

After his meal the giant took some bags of gold out of a cupboard, dumped them on the table and began to count the gold pieces very slowly and carefully. When he had finished he lay down to sleep. And now Jack could hear his tremendous snoring —it was like the heaving of mountains and the battering of waves on rocks all jumbled together. Then it was that the woman opened the oven door and whispered:

"Get out now, Jack, run off home as fast as you can."

But while the woman's back was turned, Jack grabbed one of the money-bags and ran out of the door as fast as his legs could carry him. On he ran down the path as fast as the wind, not daring to look back. Then he stepped on to the beanstalk and scrambled down step by step until he got to the garden. He rushed into the kitchen and emptied the gold coins on to the table just where his mother was having her bit of breakfast.

"What's all this?" asked the poor widow. "I thought you were still in bed, too ashamed to come down after what happened yesterday."

Breathlessly Jack told her all about the magic beanstalk and his adventure in the giant's castle.

The widow now had to admit that Jack was very much cleverer than she had thought and that selling the cow for a handful of beans had turned out to be not such a bad thing after all.

And so now Jack and his mother lived comfortably for quite a long time, until all the gold was spent. They had plenty to eat and drink and they bought lots of new clothes and things for their cottage.

Jack and the Beanstalk

But there came a day when the widow found that all the gold had been used up.

Jack secretly decided to pay another visit to the giant's castle. One fine morning he climbed up the beanstalk for the second time, got to the top above the clouds and started walking along the path that cut through the fields. When he got near the castle he hid behind a tree because he did not want to be seen by the woman. When he saw her coming out with the pail on her head he waited a moment and then slipped unseen through the open door. Then he opened a cupboard and hid inside behind all the pots and pans. But only just in time—for just then he heard the terrific thump, thump, thump of the giant's boots and though a chink in the door Jack saw him come in carrying several calves and goats over his shoulder. The giant gave a tremendous sniff and bawled:

> *"Fee foh fi fum*
> *I smell the blood of an Englishman.*
> *Be he alive or be he dead*
> *I'll grind his bones to make my bread."*

"I can smell that boy again," he roared. "Where is he?"

"I wish I knew," replied the woman. "I'd give the little rogue what for!"

But they couldn't find Jack anywhere, for he was hiding inside a great saucepan in the cupboard.

So grumbling and grunting the giant sat down at the table to eat his breakfast and when he had finished he said:

"Woman, bring me the hen that lays the golden eggs."

Out she went into the yard and presently returned with a handsome white hen which she put on the table in front of the giant.

"Lay," shouted the giant to the hen. And through the chink in the cupboard-door Jack saw the hen lay an egg of pure, solid gold. The woman put the egg safely away in the giant's money-bags and the giant promptly fell asleep and snored so loud that the whole castle shook to its foundations.

Jack waited till the woman had gone out of the kitchen, then slipped quietly from the cupboard, snatched up the magic hen and rushed out. It was not until he got through the cloud that he heard the giant's great boots come clattering after him. The giant must have heard the hen squawking a little and so had started to run after Jack. But he was too late to catch him and when Jack disappeared into the white cloud the giant gave up and went back to the castle in a raging fury.

Down the beanstalk came Jack, down into the garden and straight into the kitchen where his mother was having her bit of breakfast.

Before she could finish her mouthful he placed the hen on the table and said "Lay!" and out came a beautiful golden egg. His mother nearly choked with surprise and delight.

"Why, we shall have enough money for the rest of our lives if this wonderful hen goes on laying like this!" she exclaimed. She felt more pleased than ever with Jack for having exchanged their cow for a handful of beans.

But not many months passed before Jack's taste for adventure got the better of him and he felt he must climb yet a third time up the beanstalk. Again he said nothing to his mother but got up early one morning and started his climb, wondering what he would get this time from the giant's castle.

When he reached the top he walked very carefully through the white cloud and stopped at the beginning of the path that led through the field, just to make absolutely sure there was nobody around. Then he started to walk briskly until he arrived at the castle. But he found that the usual door was closed and on turning the knob he discovered that it was locked. So he walked round to the back but only just managed to dodge out of the way of the woman, who was coming out of a shed with the milk-pail on her head. He ran back to the front and to his horror saw the enormous figure of the giant striding with huge strides down the path. Luckily for Jack there was a beautifully-branched tree growing alongside the castle near where he was standing and up he climbed and hid breathlessly in the thick branches. From here he climbed on to a window-sill of a room upstairs and crept through the open window and listened. Soon he heard the giant's voice bawling:

"Fee foh fi fum
I smell the blood of an Englishman.
Be he alive or be he dead
I'll grind his bones to make my bread."

He could hear the giant and the woman bustling about, opening and shutting doors and cupboards and ovens, trying to find him. Then he heard them coming up the stairs, but Jack was out in a flash and safely perched himself on a branch well hidden by the leaves. When the giant and the woman were in the bedroom Jack nimbly climbed down and went through the front door, which was now half open, and slipped straight into the kitchen cupboard. And here he hid behind an enormous baking-pan.

Then he heard them clumping down the stairs, the giant moaning and grumbling all the time.

"Well, are you satisfied now?" asked the woman. "We've looked all over the castle. It's just your imagination. I'll bring you your harp so that it can soothe you to sleep, and when you wake up you'll feel better."

She went out of the kitchen and came back presently with a harp which she placed on the table.

"Play," said the giant to it, and it began to give forth the most enchanting music without anybody touching its strings.

Jack and the Beanstalk

"Ah, that will be a nice present for Mother," thought Jack. And as soon as the thundering snores of the giant began to make the castle go all a tremble, out crept Jack, snatched up the harp and was out of the castle like a shot.

But something very unexpected happened. The harp began to cry: "Master, master, somebody's taking me away! Master, save me, save me!"

Instead of throwing the harp down, Jack ran all the faster, dashed through the cloud and started to climb down the beanstalk. When he was at the bottom he felt the beanstalk swaying most dangerously from side to side. It was the giant climbing down after him!

"Mother, Mother, get me an axe quick," shouted Jack. And only just in time the old widow came running out with a hatchet. Chop! Chop! Chop! went Jack. Down came the beanstalk and with it the giant! He crashed into the garden, broke his neck and that was the end of him.

So now with the hen that laid the golden eggs and the harp to keep them entertained, Jack and his mother had everything they needed. And so they lived happily together for the rest of their lives.

The Cow, the Duck and the Pig

————————————————✱————————————————

Once upon a time a Cow, and a Duck, and a Pig lived in a comfortable farmyard.

"Moo," said the Cow.

"Quack," said the Duck.

"Grumph," said the Pig.

Every morning early, Jenny, the farmer's daughter, brought them their breakfast.

Hay for the Cow.

Bran for the Duck.

Swill for the Pig.

And they were very happy and contented.

But one day Jenny, the farmer's daughter, was taken ill, and in her place came her little brother, Joey, to feed the animals. He was angry at having to do the work when he wanted to fly his kite on the hill, and so pretended to be more stupid than he was and gave—

Swill to the Cow.

Hay to the Duck.

Bran to the Pig.

The Cow tried the swill and couldn't bear it. The Duck took a mouthful of hay, and it made her cough horribly. The Pig, who ate everything, bolted down the bran, but it was very dry to his taste, and it didn't make him feel fed at all.

The Cow, the Duck and the Pig

However, they were good-tempered souls, and prepared to overlook this sort of thing for once. But the next day Joey was just as careless. He gave the Swill to the Duck, the Bran to the Cow, and forgot to feed the Pig at all.

"Bother!" said the Cow.

"Dash!" said the Duck.

They met together in the yard, and decided to give Joey one more chance, though the Pig said he wasn't sure he even deserved that. But on the next day there was a lovely whirling wind playing round the hilltops, and Joey rushed away to fly his kite, and no one got anything at all.

"I am hungry," said the Cow.

"I am very hungry," said the Duck.

"I am going to faint," said the Pig.

They stood disconsolate in the yard, while the big white clouds sailed over their heads from east to west, and the leaves sang in the wind. And just at that moment a Fairy walked in through the yard gate. He didn't look much like a Fairy—in fact, anybody who saw him would have said he was a Tramp: his clothes were in rags, his flat brown feet were bare, and his hair was full of hay stalks. But the Cow, and the Duck, and the Pig knew at once who he was, and greeted him enthusiastically.

"Thank goodness it's you!" said the Cow.

"You have come just in time!" said the Duck.

"Give me something to eat!" said the Pig.

The Fairy smiled, and asked what the trouble was. "That's bad," he said when he heard. "But never mind, it's not so bad that something can't be done. Perch on my shoulder, Duck. Get under my arm, Pig. And hold on to my coat-tails, Cow." They did as he told them and then somehow or other (mind you, that Tramp really was a Fairy), they all disappeared from the farmyard and never appeared again until they reached the middle of a little forest five miles away, where there was a green

The Cow, the Duck and the Pig

grass clearing, and a charcoal burner's hut. And, best of all, there was a load of hay for the Cow, a dish of bran for the Duck, and a great big, big pail of swill for the Pig. "Now stay here and eat," said the Fairy, "and I will come back for you at sunset."

"Umm," said the Cow, with her mouth full.

"Umm, umm," said the Duck, with her beak full.

And the Pig was too busy to say anything at all. So he wiggled his curly tail to show that he, too, agreed.

Then the Fairy disappeared again, and reappeared just behind a hedge on the hilltop where Joey was flying his kite. He whispered a magic word to the wind, and it immediately gave a great puff, which nearly tore the kite string out of Joey's hand, and then began to pull him, willy-nilly, over the hill. He wanted to let go, but found that he couldn't, and so was forced, helter-skelter, after the kite, through hedges which scratched his face, over muddy ploughed fields which tore his shoes off, and he was finally dropped—splash! splosh!—into a green scummy pool in the valley. He scrambled out and made his way home, and when his mother saw him she stripped off his wet clothes, spanked him soundly for losing his shoes, and put him to bed with no dinner.

"Good!" said the Fairy, who was hiding behind the kitchen door. "And now to cure poor Jenny."

He went into the fields and picked a handful of cowslip flowers; then he went into the woods and pulled up a handful of green moss; then he went to a fairy spring that nobody knows about, and filled an acorn cup with water. With these he made a Magic (which all the Doctors in the world would pay a lot to know about), and just before sunset he slipped into Jenny's room, where she was lying, feeling dreadfully bad, and so softly that she never even felt it, he dropped the Magic on her forehead. Immediately her head stopped aching, and she fell soundly asleep.

The Cow, the Duck and the Pig

At sunset the Cow, and the Duck, and the Pig woke up after a satisfying rest, to find themselves back in their own farmyard.

"That's funny," said the Cow.

"I thought——" said the Duck.

"Anyway, I feel much better," said the Pig.

And on the next morning, to their great delight, out into the yard, all aglow in the sunshine, stepped their beloved Jenny. She looked more beautiful than ever, and, best of all, she brought them their right breakfast.

"Moo," said the Cow.

"Quack," said the Duck.

"Grumph," said the Pig.

Chanticleer and Pertelotte

---------------------*---------------------

Once upon a time there lived a poor old widow and her two daughters in a little cottage by the meadow.

She had a small farm with some pigs, a cow called Daisy, a sheep called Molly, seven fine-looking hens and a magnificent rooster called Chanticleer. He really was a grand-looking bird, with a comb as red as flaming fire, a coal-black beak and feathers glowing bright with many colours. How fine he looked as he strutted proud and upright in the farmyard.

No other rooster in the land could crow as loudly or as beautifully as Chanticleer, and the old widow and her two daughters were very proud of him.

One night Chanticleer had a strange dream and it worried him so much that he woke up his wife Pertelotte to tell her all about it.

"I've had a really nasty dream, my dear," he said. "I was walking up and down the yard when I saw a strange animal come racing towards me. It was a brownish-reddish colour, but it had a kind of black fur above its eyes and its long bushy tail was jet-black too. Its eyes gleamed like coals of fire and just as it was about to seize me in its jaws I woke up."

"Shame on you, husband," cried Pertelotte. "Fancy a great strong rooster like you being afraid of dreams. Dreams don't mean a thing." And she closed her eyes and went back to sleep again.

Chanticleer and Pertelotte

Chanticleer felt a wee bit ashamed, but though he didn't bother Pertelotte any more he feared secretly that his dream might come true.

The next morning Chanticleer was strutting proudly round the farmyard followed by Pertelotte and the six hens. But not very far away in a bed of cabbages, a big red fox lay in hiding, waiting to pounce upon Chanticleer. Chanticleer had

strutted on ahead of the hens and suddenly he caught a glimpse of the fox's face. It reminded him of the animal he had seen in his dream and he was just about to run away when the sly fox called out:

"Good morning, Sir Chanticleer, don't run away. I am your friend and I was the friend of your father before you. Whenever I hear your fine voice crowing in the morning I remember your father, who had a wonderful voice like yours. He often used to sing to me when I asked him to, for I did admire his voice. You could hear it for miles around, over hill and dale, just like yours. Won't you please sing for me, just this once? Just like your dear father did, with your eyes tightly closed, standing on your tip-toes and your neck stretched right out. Please sing for me, just this once, Sir Chanticleer."

You may well imagine Chanticleer was delighted to hear all these nice remarks about his voice, for he was secretly very proud of it and thought there was no other rooster to compare with him. So for the moment he forgot all about his bad dream and his fear of the fox, and he said:

"Yes, Mr. Fox, I will sing for you."

And so standing high upon his toes, and stretching his neck right out, and closing his eyes tight, and opening his coal-black beak, he began to sing with all his might: "Cock-a-doodle-doo!"

At that instant the sly fox leapt up at him, grabbed him by his neck, flung him over his back and raced off into the woods.

When Pertelotte saw that her beloved Chanticleer had disappeared she started cackling at the top of her voice and running this way and that in great excitement. And all the other hens started to do likewise. And when the old widow and her two daughters heard all the noise in the farmyard they too came running out. And they all started running after Mr. Fox, whom they could see galloping off in the distance with Chanticleer flung over his back. Soon they were joined by the ducks and geese from the pond and all the bees from the bee-hives, and by Talbot and Shaggy, the two collie-dogs belonging to Farmer Giles, the next door neighbour, and by Farmer Giles himself. And his two farm hands, Jenkins and Humphrey, joined in the chase, shouting fearful cries and waving long sticks in the air.

And when Chanticleer saw all the great crowd that was chasing Mr. Fox, he took courage and said to Mr. Fox:

"I say, Mr. Fox, why don't you turn round and tell all those silly people not to be so stupid. Just turn round and tell them that you mean to eat me up no matter what *they* do or say. Tell them you'll soon be safe in your lair and that they'll never be able to catch you." When Mr. Fox heard this he said:

"How right you are, Sir Chanticleer, I shall certainly do so."

But the moment he opened his mouth the rooster jerked himself away and flew high up into the nearest tree.

And Mr. Fox, seeing that he had made a great mistake in opening his mouth, called out to Chanticleer:

"Come down, my friend. I'm sorry I scared you. I must have grabbed you too hard when I caught hold of you. Come down again, I won't hurt you this time."

But Chanticleer was not to be fooled again. And turning to Mr. Fox he said: "Oh no, Mr. Fox, you'll never get me again. You'll never catch me again with my eyes shut." And then he flew down and ran back to Pertelotte and the old widow. And everybody was very happy to have him back safe and sound once more.